AH POOK IS HERE
AND OTHER TEXTS

AH POOK IS HERE
and other texts

The Book of Breeething
Electronic Revolution

by

William S. Burroughs

JOHN CALDER • LONDON
RIVERRUN PRESS • NEW YORK

Ah Pook Is Here and Other Texts first published in Great Britain 1979
by John Calder (Publishers) Ltd.,
18 Brewer Street, London W1R 4AS

Ah Pook Is Here first published 1979 by John Calder (Publishers) Ltd., London

The Book of Breeething originally published 1974 by OU Press, Ingatestone, Essex

Electronic Revolution originally published 1971 in *The Job*, Grove Press, New York

The Book of Breeething © William S. Burroughs and Robert F. Gale, 1974

BRITISH LIBRARY CATALOGUING DATA
Burroughs, William, b. 1914
  Ah Pook is here, and other texts.
  I. Title II. Burroughs, William, b. 1914.
  TV The book of breeething III. Burroughs,
  William, b. 1914. Electronic revolution
  818'.5'408   PS3552.U75

ISBN 0-7145-3683-0
Library of Congress Catalog   No. 80-460124

Typeset by Specialised Offset Services Limited, Liverpool

Contents

Preface

Ah Pook Is Here was originally planned as a picture book modelled on the surviving Mayan codices. Malcolm McNeill was to do the illustrations, and I was to provide the text. Over the years of our collaboration there were a number of changes in the text, and Malcolm McNeill produced more than a hundred pages of artwork. However, owing partly to the expense of full-color reproduction, and because the books falls into neither the category of the conventional illustrated book nor that of a comix publication, there have been difficulties with the arrangements for the complete work – which calls for about a hundred pages of artwork with text (thirty in full-color) and about fifty pages of text alone.

The book is in fact unique. Some pages are entirely text, some entirely pictorial, and some mixed. Finally Malcolm McNeill and I have decided to publish the text without the artwork, still in hopes of seeing the eventual publication of this work that has been eight years in preparation.

William S. Burroughs
27 April 1978

AH POOK IS HERE

Foreword

The Mayan codices are undoubtedly books of the dead; that is to say, directions for time travel. If you see reincarnation as a fact then the question arises: how does one orient oneself with regard to future lives? Consider death as a dangerous journey in which all past mistakes will count against you. If you are not orienting yourself on sound factual data, you will not arrive at your destination or in some cases you may arrive in fragments. What basic principles can be set forth? Perhaps the most important is relaxed alertness, and this is the point of the martial arts and other systems of spiritual training – to inculcate a psychic and physical stance of alert passivity and focussed attention. Suspicion, fear, self-assertion, rigid preconceptions of right and wrong, shrinking and flinching from what may seem monstrous in human terms – such attitudes of mind and body are disastrous. See yourself as the pilot of an elaborate spacecraft in unfamiliar territory. If you freeze, tense up, refuse to look at what is in front of you, you will crack up the ship. On the other hand, credulity and uncritical receptivity are almost as dangerous.

Your death is an organism which you yourself create. If you fear it or prostrate yourself before it, the organism becomes your master. Death is also a protean organism that never repeats itself word for word. It must always present the face of surprised recognition. For this reason I consider the Egyptian and Tibetan books of the dead, with their emphasis on ritual and knowing the right words, totally inadequate. There are no right words. Death is a forced landing, in many cases a parachute jump. The motor sputters ominously. Look around for a place to land. The landscape is deceptive. What appears from the air as a smooth field may turn out to be quicksand or swamp mud. Conversely, a mountainous area may contain a hidden valley or a smooth plateau. Focus attention. Look with your whole body. Pick your spot and land in the dark. *Blackout.*

Death must bring a measure of forgetfulness. Consider the Mayans, cut off in a small area; too much knowledge of death could remove the essential ingredient of oblivion. Death is always regression, a moving backwards to infancy and conception. So why stop there? They had to keep moving further and further back. Otherwise death would be remembered, and death remembered ceases to be operative. Finally they moved back four hundred million years. Who or what was there that long ago? Obviously, such time spans have no meaning in terms of actuality. However, in terms of remembered time, such calculations show how far they had gone in the direction of remembering death. Consider the social structure: a small percentage of priests who could read the books and make calculations on the calendar, and a large percentage of illiterate workers. The workers must have served as a reservoir into which the priests could reincarnate themselves and re-emerge into the priest caste, identified by certain signs after the Tibetan system.

Time has no meaning without death. Death uses time. This is a cumulative process so that time is used up faster and faster. There is an exact parallel here with inflation, since money buys time. So it takes more and more to buy less and less. How did the Mayans react to this impasse? By back-dating time. Like this: the dollar is worth, say, one-fifth of what it was worth fifty years ago. So we back-date money fifty years. Then a hundred years, and so forth, moving backwards in time. Eventually we come to a point where there was no money so we are back-dating the concept of money – the concept of time.

The workers could not read the books and undoubtedly they were prevented from learning. Had they been able to read the books they would have learned to remember, to familiarize themselves with death and identify with death.

This would have conveyed immunity. Death is a virus and the Mayan books are a vaccine. Death is represented in the codices by one spot of decay through a series of shadings to skeleton figures. In short this is gradient exposure. Also familiarity with death and consequent immunity is conveyed by actual copulation. A glyph depicts the Moon Goddess copulating with a death figure, and we may assume that the books destroyed by Bishop Landa contained many such scenes.

Time is that which ends. Time is *limited time* experienced by a sentient creature. Sentient of time, that is – making adjustments to time in terms of what Korzybski calls neuro-muscular intention behaviour with respect to the environment as a whole ... A plant turns towards the sun, nocturnal animal stirs at sun set ... shit, piss, move, eat, fuck, die.

Why does Control need humans?

Control needs time. Control needs human time. Control needs your shit piss pain orgasm death. So what does Control intend to do with this commodity that will be so smart? Like the Mayan priests they intend to use human time to make more time.

If time is that which is experienced by a sentient being, then death for that being is the end of time. And with death as zero, checks for any amount of time can be written by adding zeros. Even if there is some memory of past lives, the being has no way of knowing if he has been dead four seconds or 400 million years. These checks would seem to be overdrafts in that they are back-dated to a time when the checks the bank and the depositors did not exist. They bear however the signature of death, which is interruption of sentience.

I have spoken of the transitional forms of death and the identification of the death organism with the dying. This identification may take the form of actual copulation with death. Death, who can take either male or female form, fucks the young Corn God and the Corn God ejaculates 400 million years of corn from seed to harvest and back. This operation requires actual corn and an actual human body to represent the young Corn God. This then is an *endorsed* check signed by the young Corn God. Once he has signed the check any number of zeros can be added. The Mayan time bank operated on these endorsed checks. Death is accepted by the dying.

Now consider present time and the proliferation of *unendorsed* checks ... air and car crashes, wars, fires, accidents, random deaths. These checks are good only for *the actual time covered*. A hundred thousand deaths may buy a million years, but there is always more and more human stock to consume time. The present-time impasse is less and less qualitative time for more and more people. Finally no qualitative experience, just random time computed on a purely quantitative basis. Ultimately time will be exhausted.

The Mayan system is the exact opposite. Less and less people for more and more precise written time. One system leads to an excess of mortals and a shortage of Gods; the other to an excess of Gods and a shortage of mortals. In either case, to a dead end. In the case of the present system the cycle of increased population, increased pollution, less and less to feed more and more, is now apparent. So attempts are made towards restoration of qualitative experience: meditation, communes, ecology, bio-feedback, est, encounter groups, magic – in short, transcendence. This is patchwork after the fact. The damage is already done, and the deadly formula of proliferation is already irreversible. These measures, even if successful, would then lead to the Mayan impasse.

And what measure could the Mayans have taken? They could have expanded, colonized, increased population to ensure human reservoirs. This then would lead to the present impasse. Also they were becoming less and less able to expand, just as the present system with its proliferation of a low-grade human product is becoming less and less able to assimilate anything else. Consider the possibility of Mayan endorsed checks erupting in Present Time. This could lead to virgin soil epidemics, reducing the population to Mayan proportions, and finally to the Mayan impasse. Similarly, the dumping of unendorsed checks onto the Mayan market would lead to the expansion and proliferation of population and the present impasse.

Time is that which ends. The only way out of time is into space. Why did the Mayan priests need human bodies and human time? Wait. They needed these bodies and this time as a landing field and as a launching pad into space. They required actual corn and a human Corn God.

William S. Burroughs
20 September 1975

HIROSHIMA ... 1945 ... AUGUST 6 ... 23 SECONDS
BEFORE 8 A.M.

Boy opens sex magazine ...
Young Japanese couple fucking to count down ...
Two boys jacking off to count down ...
23 WHEEEEEEEEEEEEEEEEEEEEE ...

A BLINDING FLASH OF WHITE.

I put the following questions to CONTROL:
    Question: Bombing incident after sexual virus?
    Answer: Yes.
    Question: Was it to obtain such an incident that the bomb
was dropped on Hiroshima?
    Answer: Yes.
    Question: Who really gave that order?
    Answer: CONTROL.

The Ugly American ... The instrument of CONTROL ...

You see, I was building up an identikit picture of the man ...
probably a Mayan scholar ... certainly rich ... obviously
obsessed with immortality ... Perhaps a Rosetta Stone exists.
Perhaps some of the codices survived the book burnings of
Bishop Landa. Could this man have discovered those books
and learned the secrets of the Mayan Control Calendar? The
secrets of fear and death? And is this terrible knowledge even
now computerized and vested in the hands of far-sighted
Americans in the State Department and the CIA?

'Put that joker DEATH on the line. Take care of Mao and his gang of cutthroats.'

I decided to call him John Stanley Hart.

Even as a child the thought that his being could ever STOP gave him a terrible feeling and filled him with a grim unchildlike resolve.

'*I will live forever*' he decides. Across the room the new servant drops a vase of flowers on the floor. He stands there and watches her clean it up. A pale fishy child cold as ice – few are at ease in his presence. He already has the power to make things jump out of other hands. As he grows, the power to make fear grows with him and the fear of others covers him like a heavy gray cloak.

Here he is at Harvard. He despises the other students. They are human animals and they will die. He dedicates himself to immortal studies. The Egyptians were also obsessed with immortality. Perhaps they found something out. He studies the Egyptian hieroglyphs and reflects that a way must once have existed to revive the rich mummies in immortal forms. Rather like going in deep freeze, which he has of course considered. Suddenly a picture flashes in front of his eyes ... In a forgotten crypt the last papyrus with the revival formula crumbles to dust. The suffocating horror of that blind alley closes around his heart like ice.

'*Dead forever*' he groans. '*Oh God, think of it – me in deep freeze and nobody to thaw me out ...*'

He collapses sobbing and whimpering in abject terror. But young Hart comes of good stock. He pulls himself together. He will avoid these deadly snares. He will learn the secrets of his predecessors and profit by their errors.

He turns now to Mayan studies. He is looking at a copy of the Dresden Codex. He glimpses the death formula. Across the table a gawky youth drops his glasses on the floor. One lens is broken.

With his first and last friend, Clinch Smith, Hart organizes an

expedition to find the lost Mayan books and gain the secrets of
fear and death.

Ruined temple in a jungle clearing. Stelae and bas-reliefs on
walls have been defaced by the death symbol crudely chiselled
across stone faces and dates. In the ruins of what had been the
inner room of the temple, Hart and Clinch Smith have lifted a
stone and found the books with a skeleton curled around them
in fetal position. The skeleton turns to dust as the books are
removed. Cut to evening shadows in the clearing indicating
lapse of time during which Clinch and Hart have had time to
study the books ...

Clinch Smith stands there all square-jawed and noble:
'Perhaps this will show a way beyond death ... open a new
frontier for adventurous youth ... It belongs to humanity,
John.'

'Don't be a fool, Clinch. With this knowledge we can rule
the planet.'

'*They* didn't do so well, John.' Clinch gestures to the defaced
stelae.

Hart: 'They made a mistake.' He shoots Clinch three times
in the stomach. The smoking gun still in his hand, he looks
around.

'How did this happen?'

Ghost voice of Clinch Smith: 'Death asked to be paid in
kind, John.'

Hart arrives at police post with Clinch Smith draped over the
saddle of his horse.

Cop: 'Un venado Commandante.' (A deer. This expression
for someone who has been killed is peculiar to rural Mexico
where the deceased is usually brought into a police post
draped over a horse like a deer.)

Hart: '... Mi amigo ... asesinado para bandidos ...'

Commandante spreads out pictures on the desk. Hart picks
out three of the youngest bandits ...

Ah Pook: 'And show some respect ...'

Seed God: 'There's a lady in here ...'
STOP ... LOS ALAMOS ... U.S. MILITARY
RESERVATION AUTHORIZED PERSONNEL ONLY
Young Corn God: 'Take off the hat gringo ...'
Ah Pook: 'And show some respect ...'
Baby Corn God: 'There's a baby in here ...'
Mr. Hart: 'They died bravely ...'
Commandante: 'It is their trade señor ...'

Train whistle ... train in lunar landscape of Northern Mexico
... cut to Mr. Hart's private car, books spread out on a table.
He is reading the books laboriously from a Spanish key. Here
is the young Corn God turning into DEATH ... 'When I
become *death* ... *death* is the seed from which I grow ...'
Now this dying to produce oneself sounds awfully hit-and-
miss to canny young Hart. Obsessed by his desire for
immortality, he does not grasp the full significance of this
simple survival formula nor the seeds of disaster it contains.
Mr. Hart certainly does not think of himself as a Christian, yet
all his thinking is formed by Western Christianity. He thinks in
either/or, that is, one-God terms. He is looking for *the* secrets
of fear and death. 'Must be one thing or the other' he tells
himself, 'it's all very simple – the priests became DEATH and
therefore they could not die ... Can't leave any loose ends
trailing about, though.'
'At dawn death came to the hut ... The youth tried to face
him and hurl a magic object ... He almost succeeded for *death*
was old and tired ...' The weakness of *death* in this passage
alarms him. Perhaps the priests postulating all those millions
of years in which they had existed killed themselves with old
age? Mr. Hart is not really an intelligent man. He does not at
this point even guess the real reason for these expeditions into
remote past time. The priests made calculations on their
calendar dating back 400,000,000 years. Why?

Mr. Hart will find out in time. He will find out that death
needs time. Death needs time like a junkie needs junk. And
what does death need time for? The answer is soooo simple.

Death needs time for what it kills to grow in, for Ah Pook's sweet sake, you stupid, vulgar, greedy ugly American death sucker. Like this! Death walks out in the field and kills the young Corn God. Young Corn God becomes a death seed from which another young Corn God will grow – birth and death in all its rich variety of an old outhouse. However, there is always more death than growth, even in the simplest terms of soil exhaustion. Corn is a very exhausting crop. Apparently the Mayans were ignorant of crop rotation, and in any case had no domestic animals to eat a cover crop and shit it back in fertilizer. Consequently, soil exhaustion was a problem and after the soil in the immediate vicinity of a city was exhausted, they had to travel further and further to find fertile fields, spending more and more time in transit to and from. Now every time you kill the young Corn God life goes out of him. The seed grows slower ... the seed loses vitality. The Corn God looks like a soulless zombie. And finally the seed does not grow. No time for death. So death has to travel.

Death takes the young Corn God back to a time when he hadn't been hit so often he is punch-drunk, back to his youth – back back back ... clickety clickety clack ... back to the Garden of Eden. Sure, death will burn that down too. The Mayan priests made these expeditions into past time because they had burned down present time. Mayan scholars have wondered why they did not make calculations into future time; they were overdrawn. Checks bounced. Nothing and nobody there.

Now this did not happen right away. You don't get hooked on the first shot, and even when you are hooked you can control it for a while maybe, stay on the same dose ... but fix yourself on a junkie on heroin for several thousand years. Control that habit? So he goes back to the time when his habit was manageable, and when it gets out of hand there he goes further back-back-back. Look at the Mayan pantheon and the calendar and you will see that the Mayans, as experienced vampires and time junkies, were keenly aware of this impasse and took what precautions they could to avoid it by balancing the Gods of death and life, not as Mr. Hart's accounts are balanced on an either/or basis, but through a series of transitional shadings.

Death appears also as a culture hero showing a way beyond death, and this was the aspect of death that appeared to the idealistic Clinch Smith ...

The sea chest of the dead man is in the consulate and the vice consul breaks the news to mother.

Ma Smith knows who killed her son. So does Clinch's young brother. Look at any power figure and you can see what orders he will give ... Roehm's death in Hitler's eyes ... The entire Smith clan must be eliminated ...

'No boasting like a fool, this deed I'll do before this purpose cool.' He must silence the voice of Clinch Smith forever. The entire Smith clan must be wiped out ...

Flash of Mrs. Smith dead in car wreck ... Young Guy Smith flees to South America.

'We have scotched the snake not killed it ...'

Young Guy Smith joins Audrey Carsons in a remote finca in the Andes.

Audrey Carsons: Eerie ghostly rotten vulnerable reckless he possesses at the same time the cold intelligence of Mr. Hart. He is Hart's alter ego and nemesis.

Guy Smith: He is the buck-toothed Mayan Death God before the face was broken and twisted by altered pressure, features wrenched out of focus, body emaciated by distant hungers. A face where time has never written.

Old Sarge: Has the close-cropped iron-gray hair and ruddy complexion of the regular army man. There is also a suggestion of the Polar Star God in his appearance.

In the transitional forms of Death, Death to some extent identifies with the man he kills and *shares* his death. So shared Death loses its absolute character. Death shows himself to the dying. All this seems very subversive to Mr. Hart, who never identifies with his victims. To do so would put him in danger of becoming a victim himself. Yet at some point death must take this risk. He must become a mortal and die in order to be reborn. Mr. Hart wants to *be* death but he will not *know* death. Death will not serve a stranger who cannot prove his title, a gringo who fears the very word and sets up a house rule that the word 'Death' may not be pronounced in his presence. Hart cannot *read* the Mayan books. He is reading them as one who reads Moby Dick to find out about whaling and to hell with Ahab, White Whales, Quequod and Ishmael ... What is written there long dormant is now a virulent strain of virus waiting to escape, to leap from the pages and infect millions of human hosts, not with Mr. Hart's greedy Bible-belt 19th-century capitalistic message, but with their own messages, cruel, tender, ambiguous, shameless, slimy, virginal, capricious, immeasurably old and ravenously young ... Mr. Hart, who would be Death, does not know to whom he is aspeak.

Rainbow Valley in the Bolivian Andes. Young Guy Smith and his friend Audrey Carsons are studying in the Death Academy under experienced instructors. They are learning to fly on the wings of death. They are learning what Mr. Hart is afraid to know, taking the risks he is afraid to take.

Two bandits stand against wall ... 'When the bullets hit, muchachos, it is like sucking for breath that does not come. Do not brace yourself and stick out the chest. *Spread* yourself against the wall and relax the shoulders ...'
   Old Sarge: 'Now a firing squad is something you expect and prepare yourself for ... How about unexpected bullets? Casualty figures we call them in the army ...'

Audrey and Guy move into a bombed-out village, taking cover ... Viet Cong? Americans? Germans? They are soldiers in battle. A shot – Audrey falls. Guy whirls and gets the sniper in a window. He drags Audrey behind a wall. One look at Audrey's face is enough. You can't mistake that gray shadow spreading up the face as the gray lips move.

'I thought I heard another shot close by …'

Death is very close now and Guy can smell it. It's a gray smell that stops the heart and cuts off the breath. Smell of the empty body. Smell of field hospitals and gangrene. A smell you could *see* in Audrey's face *before* the bullet hit …

Ernest Hemingway could smell it on others. Here he is in a jeep with General Lanham, known as Bucky to his friends, and Ernie was a real general lover. It's worse than being a cop lover.

'Have to relieve that man' says Bucky.

'Bucky' says Ernie, 'You won't have to relieve him. He won't make it. He stinks of death.'

When the jeep reached Regimental Command Post, it was stopped by Lieutenant Colonel John Ruggles.

'General …' said Ruggles saluting. 'The Major has just been killed. Who takes the First Battalion?'

Question: What is the presence here that Ernest could smell?

Answer: The presence of death. Death is an organism with many disguises and many smells. Here it is *gray*. A gray being whose face is not clear.

Question: He is killing you?

Answer: Not by any action beyond his presence … His presence has released a gas … It's a dull smell … dull and faintly metallic … a taste too … a gray dead taste in the mouth … I can't breathe in this smell …

The train stops in a desert ghost town … empty station … water tower. Mr. Hart glances out the window. The gray Vulture God leans against a wall, one knee out, his face shaded by a sombrero. Mr. Hart begins to cough and covers his face with a handkerchief.

The train starts. Mr. Hart recovers and resumes his study of the Mayan books as the scenery outside abruptly changes and the train winds through a river valley of meadows, fields and trees.

Like the Egyptian and Tibetan books of the dead, the Mayan books chart the area after death and the ambiguous no man's land between death and rebirth. The Tibetan and Egyptian books stress formalized ritual; if you say the right things to the right Gods everything will be all right. The Mayans on the other hand mapped an admittedly dangerous and largely unexplored area where prayers and mantras and name-dropping may not serve your cause this evening.

'I happen to be a good friend of Osiris if that name means anything to you.'

The Death Cop slaps him back and forth across the face.

'Any son of a bitch tries to scare me with the people he knows ...'

'I want the American Consul ... Consul Americano ...'

Death as a Mexican cop smiles through the bars.

'No sabe Merican Consul, Meester ...'

Itzamna, Spirit of Early Mists and Showers ... Ix Tab, Goddess of Ropes and Snares ... Ix Chel, the Spider Web That Catches the Dew of Morning ... Zuhuy Kak, Virgin Fire, Patroness of Infants ... Ah Dziz, the Master of Cold ... Kak U Pacat, Who Works in Fire ... Ix Tub Tun, She Who Spits Out Precious Stones ... Hex Chun Chan, the Dangerous One ... Ah Pook, The Destroyer. Look at these poisonous color maps where flesh trees grow from human sacrifices; listen to these sniggering half-heard words of tenderness and doom from lips spotted with decay ... Death pees with decayed fingers ... the youth with erection kneels in a dog's soul, caught in her ropes and snares to be reborn as a dog ... the gray dog in rotten flesh leans against the wall, erogenous sores cover his face ... a hand ... slow decayed fingers ... hideous crab and centipede Gods surface from black seas of lightless time ... in rotten flesh gardens languid boys with black smiles scratch erogenous sores ... diseased, putrid, sweet, their naked bodies steam off a sepia haze of choking vapors. Mr. Hart coughs violently and covers his face with a handkerchief. The Polar Star God as a pullman porter knocks on the door of Mr. Hart's drawing room.

Mr. Hart: 'Yes? What is it?'

Porter: 'Your tea sir. You ordered it for five o'clock sir ...'

Mr. Hart mutters to himself ... 'Five o'clock? It couldn't be later than three ...' He looks at his watch and finds out it is five o'clock. He calls to the porter: 'All right' and opens the door, covering the books with a napkin. The porter sets out tea, pours a cup for Mr. Hart and retires. Mr. Hart looks out the window.

The train is stopped on the outskirts of a red brick river town. A travelling carnival has been set up. In a booth directly in front of the train window the Vulture God stands in front of a youth in a dog mask. The youth kneels with an erection. The Vulture God sniggers, covers his mouth looking sideways at Mr. Hart, imitating Mr. Hart coughing. The youth is spattered with decay in the next booth ... the dog mask mashed into his face ... Next booth he is naked. His head is shaved and a tuft of hair sprouts from the crown. His face had been beautiful at some other time and place, now broken and twisted by altered pressures, the teeth stick out at angles, features wrenched out of focus, body emaciated by distant hungers. The skin is white as paper, hairs black and shiny stir on his skinny legs as he fucks a black woman in a kneeling position, his body giving off a dry musty smell. And they are both humming a frequency that sets a spoon rattling in the saucer.

The booths rotate in front of Mr. Hart's window ... An aquarium booth which contains a mermaid with a snake-bird growing from the top of her head. She slides out of the aquarium through a transparent side which is made of some gelatinous material that gives and then closes as she slides through. She leaves her breasts behind and emerges as a male twin on the other side of the membrane. She steps back through the membrane and turns back into a woman. She raises her hands in a helpless gesture. A spectator leaps over the top of the aquarium and plunges into her medium where he turns into her male twin. The two twins turn bright red with pleasure and twist in rainbow copulations.

The flesh tree is encrusted with the bones of human sacrifices ... An Old God with crab claws for hands drains the sap into a stone jar with a wood tube. A force field like heat waves from his hands moulds the sap into a little man with a huge phallus ... Woman gives birth to a baby with crab claws and eyes on stalks ... Iguana and salamander babies ... Does Mr. Hart see all this? Perhaps not. He pulls down the shade. The train starts. As he resumes his study of the books many of the frames are empty.

When he gets back to New York there is not much left in his books but fear and death. He intends to occupy the space of Hunab Ku in the Mayan pantheon. Hunab Ku The One Divine ... Of him no statue or picture was made, for he was incorporeal and invisible ... He was in short the operator of the control machine and in consequence did not include himself as data ... However, having reprogrammed the machine to eliminate the troublesome 'good' Gods and those of ambiguous allegiance, Mr. Hart will soon encounter an acute time shortage. DEATH now freed from all control will use up all the TIME. And any control machine needs time ...

Question: If Control's control is absolute why does Control need to control?

Answer: Control needs time.

Exactly *control needs time in which to exercise control just as DEATH needs time in which to kill*. If DEATH killed everyone at birth or control installed electrodes in their brains at birth there would be no time left in which to kill or control.

Question: Is Control controlled by its need to control?

Answer: Yes.

Question: Why does Control need 'Humans' as you call them? (Your knowledge of the local dialects leaves literacy to be desired.)

Answer: Wait.

Wait. Time. A landing field. The Mayans understood this very well. Mr. Hart does not. He thinks in terms of losers and winners. He will be a winner. He will take it all. So he sets out to do just that. He will eliminate all unpredictable factors. He will set up the American Non Dream ... Let us look at some of the milestones in Mr. Hart's anti-dream plan ...

The Oriental Exclusion Acts: The equanimity of the Chinese is of course due to their language which allows for periods of silence and undirected thought, quite intolerable to Mr. Hart who must program *all* thought. And Mr. Hart has a bitter grudge against the Chinese involving one of the few personal humiliations of his life. Mr. Hart had taken two friends to a Chinese restaurant in New York's China Town. Mr. Hart is among other things an accomplished linguist and he has learned Chinese. After dinner he decides to demonstrate his linguistic skill and approaches an old Chinese who is sitting over a pot of tea reading his Chinese newspaper. Hart says in impeccable Mandarin Chinese ...

'The orange blossoms are blooming along the Yangtse River my friend and you are far from home ...'

The old Chinese looked up at him and said ... 'You go on you son of a bitch ...'

And after dinner on Canal Street a strange buck toothed Chinese boy in filthy white shorts sitting on a shoe shine box in a doorway looked at him with an evil knowing smile ...

'Shine Mister?'

Mr. Hart threw him a cold look and the boy made a jack off gesture ... Intolerable to think there were 500,000,000 potential terminals for such insolence. The Oriental Exclusion Acts blocked a dangerous influx and laid the way for future conflicts ... His program calls for a series of such conflicts to point up the need for a continual escalation of control measures ...

Income Tax Laws: These laws in fact close the door to extreme wealth and insure that no one acquires wealth who might use it to subvert the interests of wealth and monopoly: the interests of Mr. Hart.

Passport and Customs Control: The basic formula on which Hart's control machine rests is *unilateral* communication.

Everyone must be forced to receive communications from the control machine. It will readily be seen that any control measure expands the range of enforced communication.

The Harrison Narcotics Act: Creating thousands and finally millions of criminals by act of Congress extends police power and personnel and makes enemies of the control machine criminals by definition ... Mr. Hart is building up his control machine. He knows that DEATH is the picture of Death. Of *your* death. This is proved by the fact that there is somebody there to take the picture. Show someone the picture of his death and you kill him. Fear is the pictures of *your* fear. Show someone a picture of himself in a state of fear and you put him in a state of fear ...

Mr. Hart will burn fear down. He will use fear until it no longer produces the desired effect.

Lunar landscape ... Mr. Hart is surrounded by dogs looking at him with a peculiar snarling smile. Mr. Hart holds a whip of magnetic force fields dotted with clusters of light. He whips at the dogs and the whip stretches out lashing them with hot points of light.

'*Back back back ...*'

The dogs snarl and wince and keep coming. His whip doesn't scare them any more.

In a bombed out village, young Guy kneels besides Audrey looking at the gray dying face.

Question: Could Guy do anything for you?

Answer: He could be there that's all. Whoever is there is your helper on this one.

Question: But surely dreadful things could happen ... An old whisky priest darts out of the jungle ... Or even worse Audrey's whore who has followed him up to the front lines knifes Guy from behind and throws himself on Audie with a thump that knocks out his last breath ? ? ?

Answer: As Hemingway said 'It is very dangerous to be a man and few survive it.' It is the job of a helper to *be there*.

Old Sarge beats the chaplain out by a split second.

A Mexican kid kneels with a cup of water quicker than a whisky priest can stagger.

The fat ambulance attendant stands between her and the stretcher just so long and long enough.

Question: Audrey, you have also been electrocuted. What characterizes this form of death?

Answer: The helpers are very important on this one. They usually appear in a dream. There are three of them, little men in dark suits and gray felt hats, cold gray underworld eyes alert, unbluffed, unreadable in the yellow putty big city night faces.

'It's like this, kid ...' He hunches his back and shoots up to the ceiling in a smell of burning flesh and ozone ... 'All hunched over ... ride it out ... *Hunch* it out when it hits ... right up here kid ... We'll take over when it hits ... Gimp there can keep his hat on ... We know this run ...'

Question: Who are these helpers?

Answer: Those spirits who have survived electrocution.

At first Audrey and Guy are the only students ... Soon others come in from battlefields, plane crashes, car accidents, knife fights, OD's.

All over the world, Hart's editors bellow: *'Go out and get the pictures. The ugly pictures. If you can't find them make them. And if you can't make ugly pictures, you're just not ugly enough for this job.'*

Man has jumped from a second story window to escape fire. Impaled on an iron picket fence writhing there groaning from his ruptured guts. A fat American cop chews gum and watches impassively. The photographer is busy with light meters ...

'Pull his head back will you Mike. I want a shot of the face before the medics get here with morphine.'

The cop reaches out and grabs the man brutally by the hair and jerks his head back.

They slip through some rigs of course but Hart's photographers are well equipped to cover the real thing. Photographers are escorted by flying wedge commando units. They can cut right to the heart of a riot-torn city and get *the pictures* ... Noon market Near East backdrop ... Here is a foreign correspondent skinned alive and rolled in broken Coca Cola bottles. Rather like modern art, the end result – you know those artists who cover themselves with paint then roll around on a canvas and throw some colored plastics at it. The editor thought it was a rig at first. Good reaction faces in the crowd.

Mr. Hart sets out to be death. He learns to kill through his newspapers. He teaches his editors and newspaper owners the trick as they crawl up his ladder to where they well deserve to be.

'Now you just move this tenement fire over here and burn some more Niggers.' Chuckling over roasted babies, car accidents, explosions like a Southern lawman feeling his nigger notches.

Now these news pictures, no matter how horrible, soon wear out. They wear out because they are shown and people get used to them. Remember the Mayan books were never shown to the workers and they could not have read them in any case. Mr. Hart speaks in a cold hissing snake language into the instrument panel and the order goes out: *Go out and get those pictures. And especially the ones we can't print. If we can print them we don't want them.*

Now I will show you exactly what Mr. Hart does with the pictures too horrible to print. He reconstructs the horrible event in exact detail.

Here's one ... A South American general has captured his wife's lover, a young Air Force lieutenant. His faithful retainers hold the lover and he cuts the lover's prick off ... 'The guy kicked and kicked' ... Get his face. Get the general's face.

Mr. Hart has a keen sense of humor. It amuses him to switch these pictures on when some business rival is trying to make time with a chick.

Mr. Hart has *all the pictures*: torture, disgusting sex pictures, madness, humiliation ... Now to show how he uses these pictures to take care of anyone who gets in his way, how he can draw the pictures and the words onto *you*.

Here is Mr. Percy Jones who is experimenting with speech scramblers and tape recorders. He has demonstrated that scrambled commands act on susceptible subjects like post-hypnotic suggestions. Mr. Hart has seen enough. Jones is giving away something Hart means to keep for himself. Speech scramblers came into use around 1882 thus antedating the first tape recorder by seven years. Mr. Hart experimented with the early speech scramblers and designed his own models. The first model was a mike inside two interlocking cylinders so perforated that the speech was cut off and emerged in accordance with the perforation patterns. When he heard the first tape recorder in 1899 it all clicked into place: A way to be the VOICE inside the head of every human dog on this planet.

The first tape recorder was described as impractical and Hart saw that it stayed that way. In secret laboratories he put his technicians to work perfecting the machine so when the tape recorder hit the open market in the 1940's after World War II he was years ahead with his private research. And his research had shown him the way to control the use of this machine and discourage any experiments with speech scramblers and tape recorder cut-ups. He monopolized discoveries in this way to give himself a comfortable lead before the discovery hit the open market. You remember the American doctor in 1899 who discovered that mold could cure infections? It amused Mr. Hart to lead a newspaper crusade against the unfortunate doctor who lost his license and died in poverty while Hart's technicians experimented with mold and isolated penicillin. This he kept for his own exclusive use. He liked to think about the millions of people who could be saved by the vials stacked in his vaults. It made him feel good to think about this.

Mr. Hart has to be inhuman because humans as he calls them are mortal. And Mr. Hart is addicted to immortality. He is addicted to an immortality predicated on the mortality of others: gooks, niggers, wogs, human dogs, stinking *humans* and feeling his own inhuman contempt for these apes affords him a mineral calm. He is addicted to a certain brain frequency, a little blue note – feels so good that feeling ... he cools to metal. This cool blue frequency results from making hands tremble and sweat, from feeling the dear meritorious poor wriggle and slobber under his feet, from making people ugly and grinding their faces in it, from knowing he can squash an editor like a bug and seeing his editor know it. He needs your pain your fear your piss your shit your human body that will die and keep him alive. Plenty more where that came from, he tells himself, and that feels so good, that feeling, he could just swim in it forever and ever.

But he needs more and more stinking humans for making stuff. And what's that wonderful stuff? Well it's just feeling safer and safer. And what he digs the safest is taking care of some human cur that threatens his gilt-edge fear stock. Blue note fixes him right, just swim in it forever. Frequency results from more and more of that wonderful hands shake and sweat from knowing he can squash out fear shit.

'You see the action B.J. This soul-searching tycoon with this uh dark side to his character.'

Now for Mr. Jones.

Hart calls in the Whisperer. He can imitate any voice and make Jones whisper out the dirtiest sex words from ten feet away. He is gray anonymous and looks so much like a walking corpse that people don't look at him. They look at Jones instead. Jones goes to a newspaper stand where he has always been courteously received. The Whisperer is leafing through a magazine at the stand. The hatred that blazes in the clerk's face causes Jones to drop change all over the floor. Awkwardly he picks it up and asks for his paper in a shaking voice ... (The Whisperer is learning that voice) ... Silently the clerk hands him his change.

Jones goes into a restaurant and orders breakfast. He finishes
and lights a cigarette. A burly man at the next table looks up.

'I'm trying to eat my breakfast if you don't mind ...'

'I don't know what you mean ...'

'You know what I mean right enough you were making a
filthy noise ...'

The Whisperer sits in a corner.

Mr. Jones finally attacked a waiter who had ignored him for
half an hour. He was badly beaten and taken to a hospital and
committed to an institution for the insane.

There were many others who got in Mr. Hart's way like
that. Here is someone who is advocating the use of Vitamin A
for the common cold. He has found out that massive doses of
Vitamin A – 200,000 units taken every six hours at the first
symptom – will stop a cold or drastically moderate its course.
Mr. Hart has a vested interest in all viruses. He is busy with
virus research. Viruses like the cold sore and the common cold
can pave the way for a virus attack. This man is taken care of
as Jones was taken care of. Then Mr. Hart diverts research
into Vitamin C, which he knows is quite worthless for a cold.

There are others who advocate the use of apo-morphine for
drug addiction and alcoholism. Mr. Hart has a vested interest
in both conditions.

So they get the Jones treatment or a variation of it.

Mr. Hart turns his attention to virus as the prototype of
hostile invasion. Something *inside* you. Something you cannot
fight. How can the picture of a virus be drawn? Let us take a
simple example, the cold sore virus herpes simplex. This virus
has a crystalline hexagonal form and is fairly large. The artists
make drawings of the actual virus particle as seen under an
electron microscope. Photos of cold sores on different lips and
colors also serve as models, and the faces of those with cold
sores where you will see registered the itching, slightly
erogenous awareness that is forced upon the subject – the
constant awareness of the cold sore. A virus must always make
you aware of its presence. Draw out that cold sore feeling and
draw it in with other cold sores and cold sore faces in cold sore
virus patterns. This basic cold sore image can then be cut in

with fear images to produce a Hart cold sore ... Man with a cold sore on his lip. The ghost figure of Mr. Hart stands there feeding on the sore as the fear pictures hit and the man cowers like a frightened dog. Mr. Hart lights up with blue junk cold and blue as liquid air.

With other virus he employs the same procedure. A virus is a living picture that makes itself out of you.

Extensive experiments have been carried out on fruit flies showing the effects of radiation over many generations. None of the mutations resulting from radiation were biologically desirable, that is, tending to promote the survival of fruit flies. However, no experiments tracing the effects of radiation on the genetics of viruses have been made public. We can safely assume that such experiments have been carried out by the Biological and Chemical Warfare boys.

Exposing viruses to various forms of radiation is a cornerstone of the investigations carried out in Mr. Hart's private laboratories. He intends to create a super virus.

BOY SURVIVES RABIES: FIRST
IN HISTORY
Lima, Ohio, Dec 21 (AP)
A six-year-old boy apparently has become
the first person in medical history to
survive a case of rabies ... Michael Winkler
of Lima, Ohio ...

'*Kill that story*' Mr. Hart screams to his editors.

'Mr. Hart, it is too late. Your own communication machine is now uncontrollable.'

You can't kill that story.

And here is another story he can't kill:

International Herald Tribune June 8, 1970
'Beginning of the End'
THE SYNTHETIC GENE REVOLUTION
Washington
We now face this fact: In a laboratory at 125 University Avenue, Madison Wisconsin, a 48-year-old chemist from

India, Dr. Har Gobind Khorana, has made a gene.

'It is the beginning of the end.' This was the immediate reaction to this news from the science attaché at one of Washington's major embassies. If you can make genes, he explained, you can make new viruses for which there is no cure.

'Any little country with good bio-chemists could make such biological weapons. It would only take a small laboratory. If it can be done someone will do it ... Science fiction has a bad habit of coming true ...'

You see this hand-calling time, Mr. Hart? The whole virus principle is up for grabs. Any small country can do it. Any individual with a laboratory and bio-chemists can do it. So where is your monopoly Mr. Hart? It is broken by your own newspapers ... Mr. Hart decides that virus is an unworthy vessel. He turns his attention to electric brain stimulation – EBS.

Mr. Hart sits there wrapped in an orange flesh robe in a blue mist of vaporized bank notes. In order to enjoy this particular form of junk he must control others because this blue junk is made of fear and control. Mr. Hart has a burning down habit and he will burn down the planet. Because the more control you exercise the less time you have in which to exercise it ... See what I mean sure Eager Beaver Hart? Electric Brain Stimulation: just install your electrodes at birth and your control is now complete ... But the junk comes from exercising control, that is, from controlling somebody who *resists* or agrees to control. When all resistance is removed then what does Control control? Control needs time. Time in which to exert control. Now Mr. Hart has the world all sewed up at birth ... And where is his junk? ... The fear that falls from his eyes and displaces objects knocking plates out of hands, spilling change on the floor and the cool blue space he lives in, he doesn't need that any more. He wants to scare someone, just press a button. No trick to that. So where is your cool blue junk now? The cool feeling inside you when you see fear there in front of you? Fear of you. Mr. Hart, suffering is your refrigeration. When you carry control to its logical conclusion you eliminate suffering. You are no longer inspiring fear in others and breathing it back as junk. You can now start kicking your control habit because the walking dead are not going to give you any more charge than a tape recorder ... Yes the Mayans ran it into the ground too but they didn't do it as quick as you will or cut themselves off with a habit as hoggish as yours.

Scene shifts to the Mayan city where Clinch and Hart found the lost books ... The terrible centipede sickness hangs in the dead stagnant air over the huts and the temple and the stone streets. Soil exhaustion has turned the area that used to be cornfields around the city into a wilderness of grass and weeds. Without ploughs these fields cannot be used, so the workers must walk five miles to the fields further up the valley, and there are not many workers left. A time of famine and pestilence. A man runs out of a narrow side street and falls screaming as a heavy stone hits him in the middle of the back. His face is hideously diseased and spattered with red patches of insect flesh, and red insect hairs grow through suppurating sores. His pursuers, about ten in number, surround him and stone him to death. His broken body oozes white juice mixed with blood and larval claws. The hideous black reek of insect mutation hangs there in the hot damp air over the stone street ...

Three young men walk towards the group. Muttering sullenly, the crowd scuttles away into side streets ...

Cumhu: an iguana boy, smooth dry green skin and black eyes that seem to be all pupil where points of light glitter like opals. There is a concentration in his eyes and body that moves objects out of his way. Because he does not move inside, everything around him is moved by his presence. He carries a flint knife, a bow and quiver.

Ouab: the cat bird boy. He is Loki and Mercury. He carries a bolo.

Xolotl: a pink translucent salamander boy with enigmatic golden eyes. He moves in liquid zigzag spurts, his eyes probing ahead like search lights. He carries a little gold trident in his loin cloth with which he can deliver a paralyzing shock from electricity stored in his body.

The boys skirt the corpse gingerly and walk on through empty streets. Sullen red-rimmed eyes watch them from doorways. They leave the paved streets of the city and climb a steep trail. Here on the highlands a thousand feet over the city are a number of houses built by the priests and nobles to escape from the heat of the valley. These houses are deserted now and overgrown with vines ...

Xolotl takes the wand from his belt and follows it like a dowser through the ruined courtyards. He stops in front of a doorway. Cumhu sniffs catching the rotten metallic smell of a Painless One. These are beings who feel neither pain nor pleasure, and more and more of them are being born owing to advanced techniques of artificial insemination. They are considered as criminals since they cannot be manipulated by the books which operate on pain and pleasure. They are worthless for purposes of sacrifice as well, and the priests have put out an order to kill them all. So they take to the jungle and the highlands, to banditry and illegal trades. In addition to their inborn inability to feel pain or pleasure, most of them are addicted to a drug which immunizes them still further from pain and pleasure and protects them against the centipede sickness.

Cumhu says, 'We are friends ... We have come to buy Pilde ... We will pay in gold ...' A rustle from the dark room ... The Painless One stands in the doorway. He is a boy of twenty, completely hairless, flesh white and waxy, his eyes cold and dead as a Lesbian fish. A slight seismic tremor quivers through his flesh. He needs the Yellow Stuff. Cumhu holds a gold nugget in his hands and smiles ... The Yellow Drug is made from gold by a process known only to the Painless Ones ... They also have the secret of preparing Pilde, the dream drug that gives the user power to travel in time. Traffic in this drug is illegal and in former times had been punished by Death in

Centipede ... The offender was skinned alive and strapped into a segmented copper centipede which was then placed on a bed of red hot coals. However, the priests are no longer able to arrest offenders or invoke such penalties. More and more they keep themselves shut up in the temple, busy with their calculations, which are all out of control at this point, so that unseasonable weather has ruined the crops and the terrible plagues from the prehistoric swamps and the beginnings of life have been loosed on the populace through experimental time travel of the priests. .

The bargain is made. The Painless One brings out a covered clay jug. Cumhu gives him the gold nugget and takes the jug ... The boys settle themselves in a ruined courtyard with a pool full of rain water. Here they take the Pilde, passing around a little cup of thin gold. Strange rotten metal smells drift from the doorway where the Painless One is preparing his medicine ... Cumhu lies back, his head cushioned on a stone yoke as the drug possesses his body, dissolving the flesh in clusters of violet light ...

He is standing on the ancient steps cut in red sandstone. At the top of the steps two phallic gate posts and a ruined wall. Beyond, a great red desert dotted with black boulders ... Now clusters of violet light rain down on the steps and burst with a musky ozone smell. He draws the smell deep into his lungs and steps through the gate posts. Silence hits him like a wall. He stops gasping. Now he picks up the spoor scent ... the phallic spoor smell ... it's a dry smell ... A smell of dry rectums and genitals, a snake smell in dry places ... No urine, no excrement in this smell and yet it is unmistakably a sex smell quivering in his spine as he moves forward feeling the dry desert air on his cheek warm and electric but cool around the edges as evening shadows fall ... The spoor smell is sharper now, red and musky ... quivering, alert, sniffing he moves forward and then suddenly dodges sideways as a red snake strikes from the shadow of a boulder – it is a Xiucutl. The bite causes death in erotic convulsions ... Before the snake can coil to strike again he crushes the venomous head with his heel, and there in the snake's dry nest is the egg. He holds the egg in his hand. It is heavy and starts to sink into his flesh. He leans against the boulder faint and dizzy, strange words in his brain that catch in his throat and carry him through strange scenes ...

'After that I tried several times to find the cottage but always missed the path and wound up by some other back porch. The houses were all boarded up. One day I walked out along the track before breakfast, mourning doves calling from the woods, and there was the path and I could see the cottage in the distance. It is early September and the summer people are leaving now.
    'I hardly expect Audrey Carsons will be there. I cross the bridge over the little creek and there is the back gate creaking in dawn wind. The cottage is open and looks deserted. I push the door open and step inside ... smell of nothing and nobody there ... The furniture has been taken away. I go upstairs and stand by the window ...'
Sky, flowers, moss, picture under a railroad bridge, yellow hair in the wind standing at the window, whiffs of winter green leaves, little post card town, fading into the blue lake and sky ... points with his left hand ... the drawer stuck ... empty sky a shower of stars long ago pale hands open the door boat whistling in the harbour ... pale snake of stars across the sky the spoor smell over the water ...

Burning cities ... crowds running and screaming diseased faces ... Suddenly the crowd sees him with the egg in his hand ... Snatching up stones and clubs they run towards him screaming,
    'FEVER EGG ...'
He throws the egg into the air above their heads. It bursts, spattering their faces and arms with patches of red and orange that burn to the bone in puffs of nitrous vapor like burning film ... They fall clawing and screaming in smouldering heaps ...
    Wild youths with red gold and orange hair, their faces glowing with pimples, mill around a closed shop shutter ...

'Open up you sons of bitches ...'
'Bring out your dirty pictures.'
'We can smell them from here.'

Cobble stones thud against the shutter. Clutching a Webley Bulldog, the proprietor peers out fearfully. The kids are in an ugly mood. Must be sixty of them out there and more keep coming – they are passing up axes and hammers from a looted hardware store. He sneaks out through a back window as the crumpled broken shutters give way and the boys spill in over broken glass and window displays.

'In the back room.'

They are bringing out devices that look like pinball machines with a machine gun ...

'Hey lookit this ...'

A boy switches the machine on and points it at another youth. As the machine hums and the gun clicks the pimples burst all over the boy's face and his pants stick out at the fly.

'Hey Jimmy cut that out ... You're giving me a hard on ...'

Other youths man the machine, spraying each other ...

'Terry for the Chrissakes ...'
'I'm coming off in my pants ...'

They carry the machines out on the sidewalk and cut loose on the crowd ...

The passers by begin to fidget and hitch their coats forward.

People are rubbing themselves ... exposing themselves ...

'All right you there ... What are you doing there?'
'And here's yours constable.'

People are tearing their clothes off, fucking in doorways, taxis, shops and on the streets and sidewalks ... Police cars and cops and ambulance attendants are drawn into a twister of frenzied flesh that heaves around the statue of Eros ...

Cumhu was laughing. It was evening now and he sat up and looked around.

The Painless One sits nodding listlessly in the doorway as blue evening shadows fall across the ruined courtyard and the pool fills with rain water. Frogs are croaking. He understands now about the Painless Ones. The drug is DEATH. They were born dead and they need more and more of the drugs to stay dead. They are the souls of renegade junky priests addicted to time travel from pleasure and pain. DEATH kills in order to be reborn into pleasure and pain. But the more He kills the less pleasure and pain he can endure. Until finally he can endure none at all. In consequence what he kills is not being replaced. You see in order to replace life he must live it, that is, experience pleasure and pain, that is, identify with the host he will kill. When he ceases to identify with the host he is killing himself ...

Ixtab, spotted with decay, seduces the youth only to find that she is embracing a replica of herself. And both of them bull dykes. They look at each other in disgust. Ah Pook kills the young Corn God and Ah Pook stands there in a standoff, coming around the other way.

Cumhu confronts his father. The father is very old, his face ravaged with disease. The dead fibrous flesh is riddled with living parasites. White worms protrude from the corners of his eyes, squirming languidly ... He has insect hands that keep crawling around.

'The books my son the ancient books the sacred books ...'

'RX written by a junky croaker 400,000,000 years ago ...'

'You have been making illegal trips my son ... Indulging in extreme experience ... You will have to draw the thorns ...'

'Pull thorns through your own prick you old creep ...'

Without more words he draws a knife of rose flint with a crystal handle and kills his vile old father. He loads the books into a bag. On the way out two pot-bellied green guards bar his way and he kills them both with two arrows firing from the hip. The boys now have the books and they can travel in time. While Mr. Hart is making all the mistakes in the book the boys are moving into present time position.

Yellow evening sky under a railroad bridge
shadows fall lake and sky
points with his left hand
snake strikes from the empty sky
pale the bite of this snake of stars

the spoor smell heavy in doorways
mourning doves calling in the distance
over the little creek the egg burst
spattering our smell of nothing
that burns to the bone
in puffs of
window
sky
flowers
moss
the spoor smell sharper
red musky hair in the wind
post card town fading into
the blue shadow of a boulder
across the ruined courtyard
(Le Comte emitted a sharp cold bray of laughter)

Two boys walk down a wide street between palm trees ... ruins of Palm Beach ... The boys wear white jock straps, white sneakers, and white belts and holsters – snub-nosed .38's with mother-of-pearl handles. One is Audrey Carsons, a blond boy standing in for the young Corn God. The other boy is the buck-toothed young Death God, Chinese Mexican Mayan I don't know Japanese person sometimes young old street boy face. He is the Dib, Anubis the Jackal God. The concrete is cracked here and there and weeds grow through. The street and sidewalks on both sides are littered with palm branches, houses deserted, lawns grown over, windows broken, frames pocked with salt. The only sound is the twittering of robins, thousands of robins on roofs balconies trees benches splashing in bird baths full of rain water and leaves.

A boy on a red bicycle flashes past them, makes a wide U-turn and stops beside them, one foot on the curb. He is naked except for a red jock strap, red leather belt, and flexible black shoes. At his belt is an 18-inch bowie knife with a rosewood handle. His flesh is red as terra-cotta, smooth poreless skin tight over the cheek bones, deep set black eyes and a casque of black hair. His ears, which stick out from his head, tremble and his eyes glisten as he looks at Audrey. Audrey now sees that his body is spattered with black spots of decay. He licks his lips and says one word in a language unknown to Audrey. The Dib nods matter-of-factly.

'This Jimmy the Shrew. He been on Gold Stuff. Going rotten kick leprosy need fuck for body back to base. He fuck you now ...'

Audrey turns aside taking off jock strap. Jimmy does same. The Dib sits down on bench and picks up yellow dusty newspaper ... NATIONAL EMERGENCY DECLARED ... Jimmy and Audrey putting on jock straps ... Jimmy is almost free of the black spots now. He gets on his bicycle and says a few words to the Dib.

'He say we come to bad place ... Need clothes ... Need money ...' Jimmy rides away and turns a corner disappearing in a blaze of hibiscus ...

The two boys walk on through the empty suburbs, heading north ... The houses are smaller and shabbier ... JANE'S MASSAGE PARLOR ... ROOMS TO LET ... Shops, offices ... The robins are thinning out and the air is getting colder around the edges.

They turn a corner and a sharp wind spatters the Dib's body with goose pimples. He sniffs uneasily.

'Need clothes ...'

'Let's see what we can find in here ...'

They are standing in front of a menswear store, mannequins with knocked-down prices covered with dust like statues. The two boys go in and come out in a cloud of dust still dusting off their clothes as the Dib emerges in a blue serge suit looking like a 1920 prep school boy on vacation. Audrey wears a dark gray suit and gray fedora which give him a 1918 corner boy look ... The wind is cold, air thin in his throat ... coughing bent over he spits blood into a handkerchief. T.B. waiting at the next stop. A shabby gray man walks by carrying a parcel.

Fish smells and dead eyes in doorways, shabby quarters of a forgotten city ... streets half buried in sand, smell of the sea ... he was beginning to remember the pawn shops, cheap rooming houses, chili parlors ... An animal runs across the road in front of them. Is something between a porcupine and an opossum. The animal turns and shows its teeth in a doorway and a baby one sticks its head out of a stomach pouch and snarls too. The Dib points.

'When you see fucking Lulow that plenty bad place.'

They walk on and go into LEE'S LUNCH ... The Polar Star God takes their order for chop suey and chili con carne. He sets the food on the table with two cups of coffee in chipped white mugs ... Audrey looks around ... small time thieves, three card monte gang, a few circus people, junkies, pushers, short cons ... Audrey finishes his chop suey and peels an orange. An old Chinese is reading a Chinese newspaper. Audrey bites into a section of orange and looks at him.

'The oranges are ripening against the Great Wall my friend and you are far from home ...'

Without looking up from his newspaper the old man says ...

'Globe Hotel ...'

The Globe Hotel on a side street. The gray Vulture God behind the counter.

Audrey has another coughing fit ...

'Room?'

Spitting his question in blood ... The clerk does not answer. He hands them a key with a heavy brass tab GOLD HOTEL ... 218 North Fairbanks ...

Room 15 – typical 1920's cheap hotel room, tarnished mirror, brass bed stand, green blinds, cheap stained wood furniture ... Audrey slumps exhausted on the bed, a pillow behind his head, a trickle of blood at the corner of his mouth ...

'Gotta get out of here soon ...'

Knock at the door. Two young hoodlums: a Japanese, his face traced with phosphorescent scar tissue that glows in the dark room, eyes invisible behind violet tinted glasses ... A young black with a sincere untrustworthy face.

'You boys carrying gold?'

'That's right. Enough to fill a lot of teeth you might say ...'

The Dib takes a package out of the brief case. The package

is wrapped in heavy silver foil. He opens it to reveal a yellow powder ...

The Japanese leans forward, sniffs and nods ...

'Need spoor eggs ... Need money ...'

'Got both ...' The Black lays out five thousand dollars in hundred dollar bills and two blue eggs about the size of robin's eggs ... The Dib picks up one of the eggs and holds it up to a light.

'I never seen them like this before ...'

'New issue ...'

'How long it take to act ...'

'About ten seconds ...'

'That can be too long ...'

'It can be. You boys want to pick up some quiet iron?'

'Yeah. And some old style Painless. From the flowers ... No synch ...'

The Black smiles ...

'For your friend is it? Now I just thought to bring some along ...' He holds up a brown bottle ... 'Fifty halvies of MS. And works ...' He cooks up a shot and gives it to Audrey ... Audrey's pale face regains color. He sits up and smiles as he sees what the Japanese boy is unwrapping: two Walther P–.38's with silencers and a box of fifty shells ... Audrey and the Dib strap on the silencered pistols. The two hoodlums are ready to leave.

'You boys better move out of here in about five minutes ... As soon as we get clear ... The alarm is already out from the barrier ...'

A Hippy pad sparsely and tastefully furnished ... rice bowls ... flower arrangements ... a live ghurka lizard ... erotic 18th-century drawings on wall depicting the Garden of Eden ... beautiful Hippy couple with long blond hair preparing macrobiotic meal ...

Narcs break the door down with sledge hammers, crush the lizard underfoot, tear pictures off the wall, empty the flowers on the floor ...

Moonlight ... a dank Grecian garden ... broken urns ... pools covered with green algae ... nightingales singing ... moonlight room where two delicate Lesbians are making love ... a flying fox flits in the window and hovers over them ...

The door shatters in a cloud of mace and tear gas as the narcs rush in with gas masks. The flying fox falls to the floor and is trampled underfoot ... The two Lesbians are stripped and handcuffed.

Audrey and the Dib in Mrs. Murphy's Rooming House, room 18 on the top floor ... room with rose wall paper, smoky sunset through the window, copper lustre pitcher and basin. On the bed Audrey and the Dib have merged into a composite being spotted with decay like a ripe peach.

The narcs rush in snatching up bottles and syringes. 'WHAT ARE YOU DOING IN FRONT OF DECENT PEOPLE?'

An egg tossed from the bed spatters the lead narc with black spots of decay.

'PUT ON YOUR CLOTHES YOU FUCKING QUEERS AND CO ...' His face rots to a skull. The other narcs rush screaming from the room as another egg bursts over their heads. They turn to skeletons on the stairs ...

Cut to Mr. Hart's estate ... House Rules on a door ...

1. Every guest will appear for dinner promptly at 8 o'clock.
2. No guest will mention the word 'death' in Mr. Hart's presence.

Mr. Hart sits at his dinner table with a watch in his hand, the guest list in front of him. His finger stops at Audrey Carson's name. There is one empty chair at the table. A dead hush as the clock strikes 8 ... a tiny spot of decay appears on Mr. Hart's cheek bones ...

Back in his one-way bug-proof room nobody but nobody bugs John Stanley Hart but his reactions are not difficult to reconstruct. He is frantically daubing his face from jars and bottles ... '*Spattered me* ... right at my own dinner table ... snot-nosed punks ... I'll put the spoor stink on them ... I'll put the Whisperer on them ... I'll do something so ugly they can't believe it ...'

People die believe it very long. And before that most of them do. How the recipe discreetly seasoned fell into his hands.

(Le Comte emitted a sharp cold bray of laughter)

Mr. Hart pays a lot of attention to the letters he publishes in his newspapers, and he has a stable of letter writers ... old gentlemen in draughty clubs, yellow tusks on the wall ... long letters with statistics urging the reinstatement of hanging and flogging ... And he has some specials like Mrs. Murphy herself ... When a four-year-old boy was nearly killed by guard dogs she wrote a letter addressed to the boy in hospital:

'He should die soon ... I hope he will ...'

And what is being said here? Any guard dog kills a child deserves an extra dog biscuit. *That is what we pay guard dogs for – to protect us against children.* The eerie old Irish witch evil that floats out of that voice is something that hangs in dank gray basements with the Dutch Boy White Lead ... in the gray rooming house curtains as she calls the desk sergeant to turn in the two boys in the top floor ...

He should die soon ... A little self-satisfied smile as if she had just eaten something good and it was agreeing with her.

I hope he will ... A secret smile from a cool gray sweetness deep inside her.

Audrey and the Dib on the stairs, silencered automatics in hand as they step lightly over the skeletons of the narcs. Mrs. Murphy has emerged from her room at the bottom of the stairs to watch the boys dragged away in handcuffs, waiting there, the smile already in place.

Audrey: 'And now for the Gombeen woman ...'

(Gombeens, male or female, are an Irish species of blackmailing police informers.)

When she sees them she turns a sickly green color like a frightened octopus. Her smile freezes and starts to flap as she holds up her fink paws and mother of God the dirty old gray red hair is standing up on her scalp.

SPUT

The bullet catches her in the forehead and blows her police informer soul out the back of her head in a splatter of blood and brains.

Mr. Hart sets the police machine in motion to capture Audrey and the Dib.

Audrey and the Dib in Atlanta airport ... Audrey is crew-cut Ivy League naval reserve officer fumbling with credit cards. The Dib is his very pregnant wife, buck-toothed, glasses, braids, reading *Sex and Politics.*

'Flight 69 now boarding at gate 18, first-class passengers only...'

'That means us honey face ...'

The other first-class passengers walk ahead of them. Old Sarge is in St. Louis matron drag with his prep school son young Guy. Cumhu, Jimmy, and Xolotl are United Nations delegates. Ouab is an atomic scientist, a briefcase chained to his wrist. The others are boarding the plane, but as Audrey and the Dib walk through the gate the metal detector rings ... Guards pop out with machine guns. An FBI man screams ... 'DON'T SHOOT. WE HAVE ORDERS FROM THE PRESIDENT TO TAKE THEM ALIVE ...'

Audrey and the Dib in cockpit. P–.38's covering pilot and copilot ... 'Take this crate to St. Louis CCD.'

'I'll have to go to the end of the runway sir ...'

'No you won't. Take it off right from here across traffic.'

Wake of the plane blows the black dust back through the airport and out into the street. People are stacked in shitting, twitching heaps ... As the plane circles the field, Audrey points with his left hand as Virus B-23, surfacing from remote seas of dead time, rages through cities of the world like a topping forest fire.

'Hey! Lookit all them dead bodies!'

A top government scientist bluntly warns ... 'Virus B-23, now loose in our overcrowded cities, is an agent that occasions biologic alterations in those affected, fatal in many cases, permanent and hereditary in those who survive and become carriers for that strain, which, as a measure of survival, they will spread as far and fast as possible to destroy enemies and quite literally *make* friends ...'

Barracks outside St. Louis, Missouri, windows boarded up and overgrown with vines. Jimmy, Cumhu, Audrey, Ouab, the Dib and young Guy are sleeping on army cots.

Old Sarge: 'All right you heroes of the fever, on your feet. You are d-e-a-d and that's another way of saying you are back in the army.'

The boys and gods get up sleepily. Cumhu and Xolotl have erections.

'All right you hardon artists ...' he points to Cumhu and Xolotl. 'Get on that sack and fuck out a black mutant. Take care of Vorster and his gang of cutthroats.'

Cumhu and Xolotl shrink back. 'Intercourse between us is forbidden by an ancient covenant.'

'Keep the ancient covenant in case you're caught short. This is war. Get your ass on that sack and fuck out some weaponry.'

Sex scene is shown through expressions of onlookers. Audrey smiles and licks his lips and turns bright red. Ouab's eyes light up inside and the hair stands up on his head. Jimmy the Shrew shows his long yellow teeth and his ears vibrate. Spots of decay spatter the Dib's face. Young Guy is fascinated and horrified. Old Sarge watches impassively as he would watch a recruit assemble his M-16.

Old Sarge (philosophically): 'Biologic fission. It could louse up the universe from here to eternity ... the old game of war.'

Cumhu and Xolotl are curled around a pulsing black egg. The egg cracks and a Black Captain steps out. These beings are black all over, even the teeth, huge eyes black and shiny, the pupil glowing like a distant star with a faint cold light.

The Black Fever produces a massive allergic reaction as if the victim had been stung by a swarm of killer bees.

Mrs. Worldly sweeps into a luxury hotel, six bellboys

carrying her luggage. She is wearing a blue mutation mink coat and there are diamonds all over her. She looks imperiously at the young hotel clerk, who is Audrey Carsons.

'I'm Mrs. Worldly. I have a reservation of course.'

'I never heard of it' says Audrey flatly.

Mrs. Worldly glares at him, her face black with displeasure. *'What did you say?'*

Her face gets blacker and blacker and starts to swell. Her face neck and arms swell like balloons splitting the skin. A scream seals shut in her throat with a muffled sound as scalding shit spurts from her boiling intestines. Diamonds pop all over the lobby.

'Scrambles!' screams a buck-toothed English lord.

Mrs. Worldly falls in a heap of shitty mink steaming like a ruptured sausage. Audrey looks at her with cold disfavor.

'We don't want your type in here. Take her outside because she stinks.'

The Black Fever takes a higher toll of women than men. Through his newspapers Mr. Hart appeals to the silent majority.

'THE NIGGERS IS KILLING OUR WOMEN FOLK.'

Vast patriotic rallies are organized.

Old Sarge: 'All right Audrey, you and Ouab fuck out a red biologic on the double.'

A pink haze of porno pictures. Emaciated, comatose, spotted with decay, Audrey and Ouab curl around a pulsing pink egg. The egg splits and a red boy with female breasts steps out.

'We are known as Reddies' he says.

A sweet rotten musky smell fills the ruined barracks.

The Red Fever attacks the rage centers, producing in susceptible subjects fulminating apoplexy and massive internal hemorrhaging. At an American First rally, Reddies in Boy Scout uniforms leap onto the podium.

'A scout is clean, brave and reverent.'

They shit on the podium and wipe their asses with Old
Glory. The delegates are speechless. Their faces get redder
and redder. Blood vessels rupture, eyes pop out. Hot blood
spurting from mouth and anus, they fall in steaming piles like
boiled lobsters.

The Reddies are also equipped with scent glands under their
arms that spread the Acid Leprosy.
A tornado of vigilantes sweeps up from the Bible Belt
hanging every living thing in their path. Even horses are
hauled into the air kicking and farting. The Reddies intercept
them at Sweet Meadows, a post card valley in Wyoming.
Sepia clouds spurt from their scent glands and billow back
through the ranks of the righteous eating flesh to the bone in
puffs of nitrous vapor. The Acid Leprosy eats a hole in time.
Grass and violets grow through the bones.
The virus plagues empty whole continents. At the same
time, new species arise with the same rapidity since the
temporal limits on growth have been removed. Any sex act
can now create life. The biologic bank is open. Anything you
want, any being you ever imagined *can be you*. You have only to
pay the *biologic price*.

Guy woke up in a strange room. He was lying on a bed naked,
heavy stagnant air covering him like a soft blanket. He lay
there staring into darkness and silence smelling his body,
hearing the pounding of his heart, the gurgles of his stomach,
faint creaks and pops in his joints. He had just woken from an
erotic dream so intense it had shaken him awake like a
nightmare:
    going down very fast in a soft elevator ...
    walking towards a railroad bridge in the light of a
window ...
    packing while a boat whistled in the harbor ...
The dream ended with someone singing an idiotic cowboy
song:
    'I'm going to California
    Where they get the California blues.'

In a broken strawberry a red bat boy sprawls with his legs up. A green shrew boy with trembling ears jacks him off ...

Fish boys in sky boats towed by singing fish ...

Bird boys with fragile gliders over burning suburbs crossed with car lights ...

A fibrous plant boy rides a giant rat in a Mayan swamp and cuddles the baby Corn God.

Audrey is in an incident from his early adolescence involving initiation into a tree house gang. The members in red shorts surround him smiling and nudging each other. He has not been allowed in the tree house before. He looks around: on a shelf a stuffed owl, a plaster skull, a rubber rod attached to a wheel ... on the wall steer horns, a percussion rifle, a hangman's noose ... a saddle on a saw horse ... a battery of car horns with rubber balls ... The Mexican kid hands him a rose tea cup.

'Drink this.'

The Mexican runs his hands lightly over Audrey's fly. Audrey drains the cup. In a few minutes he feels a burning itch in his crotch and ass. The Mexican pins his arms from behind and a boy with blue acne scars pulls his pants down. His cock flips out getting hard. The Mexican claps his arms around Audrey's chest. Audrey can feel the Mexican's cock against his naked buttocks.

'Take three deep breaths and hold the last one.'

Audrey takes three deep breaths, the blood singing in his ears, and holds his breath as the Mexican clasps his arms in a bear hug around his chest above the heart and leans back pulling him up off the floor. Audrey feels himself borne towards the ceiling as he blacks out and ejaculates ...

Boys ride in the sky on birds and fish and perform perilous sexual acrobatics on a blue and pink flesh tree in a cloud of robins and blue birds ...

A boy with wings carrying a pulsing red globe soars into the sky. Others prepare to take off from the flesh tree ...

The dark room slowly filled with pink light. Guy saw that the room was circular and the light was coming from pink walls. He saw a figure standing at the foot of the bed. It was a little red boy with flaring bat ears and wings, eyes a clear pale red with dark red pupils, his body spattered with red dots like chigger bites. The boy was looking at Guy with his whole body, bat ears and wings vibrating in a red haze. His pubic hairs, the hairs on his thighs and arms and around his nipples stood erect, dripping an opalescent juice, and a sweet rotten musk steamed off his body. The lubricant drops glittering in pink light gave him the look of an elaborate ornament or some undersea creature. His pointed red penis surged erect quivering like a dowser's wand spattering Guy's body with burning red eyes. Guy gasped and his legs sprawled open seeing the boy now with his whole body and feeling his pubic and rectal hairs and the hairs on his thighs stand erect in his flesh tingling itching burning. With a quick inhuman leap, the bat boy landed between his legs.

Arms around Audrey's chest, Cumhu stands behind him pulling his pants down in his mounting excitement body flushes red and green blushes rainbows riding very fast in a car.

Do not pass when the driver is flashing.

Flesh stick turned in his ass by a boy with a blue egg growing from his back as he propels a boat with blue farts.

Boy bent over with a flute up his ass played by a balloon-cheeked musician.

The boys finger paddle. Itching and burning from the Spanish Fly, Audrey is stripped and bent over hands braced on the saddle trying to control his mounting excitement as he waits for the first paddle. Instead the thin boy with acne scars sticks the rubber rod with a wheel on the end of it up his ass turning the wheel back and forth like he was driving a car.

'BEEEEEEEEEEEEEEEEEEEEEEP.'

A chorus of car horns as he ejaculates. One boy takes a magnesium flash picture: a dark landscape crossed by car lights and lighted windows.

The pounding of his heart in an elevator getting hard ...

In the light of a window pulls his pants down ...

Boy on all fours whipped with roses spattering his body with red blotches ass a translucent rose of pulsing flesh twisting burning ejaculating roses cherries opals bird eggs and gold fish...

Boys fuck a transparent fish in an orange pod eating oranges the juice dripping from their mouths blown away in orange clouds over the ruins of Palm Beach ...

The bat boy turned his hands palm out and Guy saw that the palms were lined with the red erectile hairs tipped with pearls of lubricant. He made a pushing motion and Guy felt a pressure like reverse magnetism shove his legs up against his chest as the boy moved forward running his hands over Guy's body and the pointed penis touched his quivering rectum vibrating in the tingling hairs penetrating his flesh and his hairs growing into the boy's thighs and balls and nipples welded together covered with the erogenous lubricant his skin burning with red dots his whole body a hive of red flesh his neck tongue and lips swelling gasping choking a taste of blood in the mouth. Silver light popped in his eyes as the windows exploded in a silent burst of crystal fragments and he was flying over the ruined suburbs, a little red bat boy.

Boy with flaring bat ears bent over with a flute up his ass his body spattered with red itching hairs and opalescent acne as he ejaculates gurgles of light ...

Boys vomit blood and roses over outhouses where boys jack off spurting robins and blue birds ...

The tree house is made of blue and pink substances like translucent larval flesh. Audrey is surrounded by faces with phosphorescent metal scars, twisted with mineral lusts, eyes sputtering blue flashes. They pass him a blue fruit that pulses in his hand and leaps to his lips like a magnet. As he bites into the fruit in ecstatic surrender, a reek of ozone and a sweet metal taste burn through his body. His thighs and buttocks, nipples and neck, blush a bright peacock blue. A soft tingling noose around his chest moves up to the neck and he goes off riding across the sky on a gallows that turns into a horse tearing whinnies through his body. A blue egg growing from his spine pops butterflies blue birds and strange-winged creatures over the ruined suburbs where screaming crowds run below him.

Boys with birds flying out the ass in black and sepia puffs are eaten by a blue bird demon and shit out ejaculating in blue pods ...

Boy with quivering blue flesh is sucked into a bell under a gallows ...

The Painless One stands motionless, untouched by the chaos around him. Cumhu stands behind him and places his hands on the boy's shoulders. The concentration in Cumhu's reptilian eyes pushes the boy forward, gasping melting in a frenzy of withdrawal, he pulls his pants down. Rainbow colors flushing through his body, Cumhu fucks the Painless One and they streak across the sky like a rocket.

Boys with fragile glider jetted by nitrous farts that billow out autumn leaves and faded sepia photos ...

A boy whipped with a transparent fish sprouts fish wings ...

Flying fox boy soars above a burning tree ...

Ecstatic copulation with giant leaves and color sex photos ...

Quivering ass hole legs up spilling lawns and golf courses and frogs ...

Xolotl rides a winged frog boy from an iridescent swamp in a cloud of flying fish ...

Boys carried up in a pink balloon wave from a strawberry basket ...

Gallows with a horse blown away in orange clouds ...

Audrey and the metal pusher ride a blue-winged horse ...

Old Sarge and the Dib wave from a World War I biplane ...

Cherubim blow golden horns up the ass of boys with legs spread the scrotum a huge pink egg in which a red cock pulses ...

The eggs explode in a musky purple smell of incense and ozone, trailing clusters of violet light ...

Red brick buildings and a blue canal where the Mary Celeste floats at anchor. The boys, with sea bags and costumes of 19th century seamen, walk up the gang plank. The Garden is a red glow of ruined cities in the distance. The sails are raised and the anchor hoisted. Young Guy plays taps as the sun fades and blue twilight settles. The boat is moving. The boys wave from the rigging. An 1890 reporter rushes up.

'What about *Mr. Hart?*'

Audrey is in the crow's nest with a telescope. He points with his left hand.

Mr. Hart's deserted ruined mansion, graffiti on the walls.

AH POOK WAS HERE

Here lived a stupid vulgar son of a bitch who
thought he could hire DEATH as a company cop.

THE BOOK OF BREEETHING

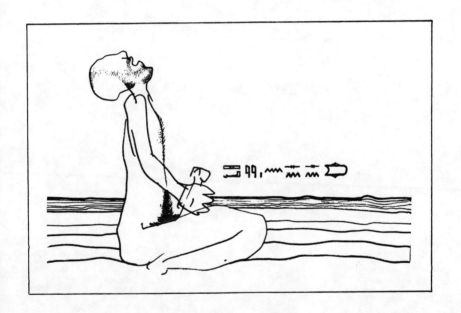

In the beginning was the word and the word *was* God and has remained one of the mysteries ever since.

What *is* word?

To ask this question assumes the is of identity: something that word essentially *is*.

Count Alfred Korzybski, who developed the concept of General Semantics in his book *Science and Sanity*, has pointed out that the is of identity has led to basic confusion in Western thought. The is of identity is rarely used in Egyptian pictorial writing. Instead of saying he is my servant they say he (is omitted) *as* my servant: a statement of relationship not identity. Accordingly there is nothing that word itself essentially *is*. Word only exists in a communication system of sender and receiver. It takes two to talk. Perhaps it only took one to write.

It is generally assumed that the spoken word came before the written word. I suggest that the spoken word as *we* know it came *after* the written word. In the beginning was the word. In the beginning of what exactly? In the beginning of *writing*.

Animals communicate and convey information. But they do not write. They cannot make information available to future generations or to animals outside the range of their communication system. This is the crucial distinction between man and other animals. Korzybski has pointed out this human distinction and described man as 'the time-binding animal'. He can make information available over any length of time to other men through writing. Animals talk. They don't write. Now a wise old rat may know a lot about traps and poison but he cannot write an article on *Death Traps in Your Warehouse* for the *Reader's Digest* translated into 17 rat languages with tactics for ganging up on dogs and ferrets and taking care of wise guys who stuff steel wool up our holes. If he could rats might well take over the earth with all its food stocks human and otherwise.

It is doubtful if the spoken word would ever have evolved beyond the animal stage without the written word. The written word is of course a symbol for something and in the case of a hieroglyphic language like Egyptian it may be a symbol for itself that is a picture of what it represents. This is not true in an alphabet language like English. The word leg has no pictorial resemblance to a leg. It refers to the *spoken* word leg. So we may forget that a written word *is an image* and that written words are images in sequence that is to say *moving pictures*. (Lest I be accused of using the is of identity I could amend the above to read that word serves *as* an image.) So any hieroglyphic sequence gives us an immediate working definition for the spoken words. Spoken words use any verbal units that refer to this sequence. If we know the script no matter what our spoken language may be we can immediately communicate in writing. A simplified pictorial script adapted to the typewriter would constitute a workable international means of communication.

Another special feature of pictorial script is that the pictures are capable of infinite variation. The English word leg has to be written in one way. A pictorial leg can be written as any number of legs.

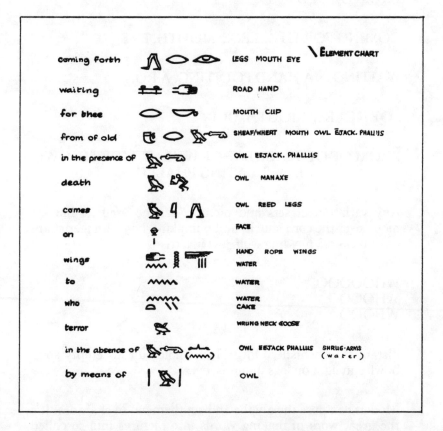

coming forth		LEGS MOUTH EYE	ELEMENT CHART
waiting		ROAD HAND	
for thee		MOUTH CUP	
from of old		SHEAF/WHEAT MOUTH OWL EJACK. PHALLUS	
in the presence of		OWL EEJACK. PHALLUS	
death		OWL MANAXE	
comes		OWL REED LEGS	
on		FACE	
wings		HAND ROPE WINGS WATER	
to		WATER	
who		WATER CAKE	
terror		WRUNG NECK GOOSE	
in the absence of		OWL EEJACK PHALLUS SHRUG·ARMS (water)	
by means of		OWL	

COMING FORTH   WAITING   FOR THEE

FROM OF OLD

COMING FORTH ... LEGS, MOUTH, EYE

WAITING ... A HAND POINTING, A ROAD

FOR THEE ... MOUTH, CUP

FROM OF OLD ... SHEAF OF WHEAT, MOUTH, OWL,
     EJACULATING PHALLUS

Any variation of sets and pictures can be used ... harvest moon over the corn shucks and pumpkins, boy with teeth bare as he jacks off, howling wolf, owl in a tree

WHOOOOO
WHOOOO
WHOOO

distant train whistle, Oliver Twist holds up his empty soup bowl, sun light on legs, mouths, eyes

Models can pose the glyphs and act them out in charades. It's the great work of making words into pictures into so called real people and places

COMING FORTH   IN THE PRESENCE OF

COMING FORTH ... LEGS, MOUTH, EYES

IN THE PRESENCE OF ... OWL
                                    EJACULATING PHALLUS

Transposing these stylized glyphs into photos and drawings
we find that there can be any number of representations of any
glyph, any number of COMING FORTHs or IN THE
PRESENCE OFs.

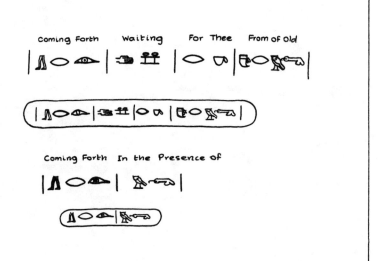

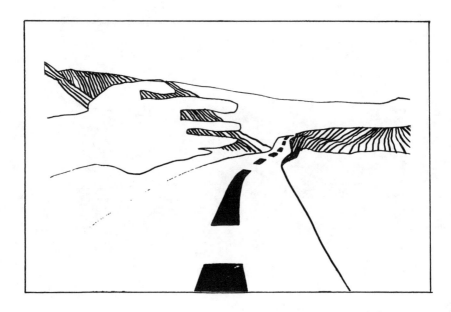

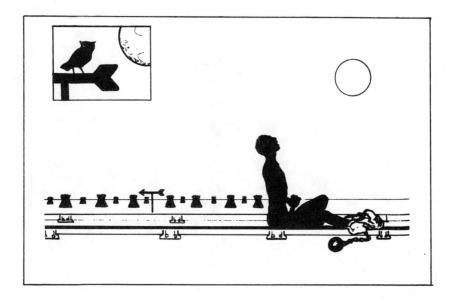

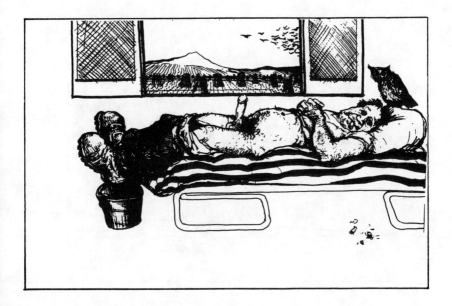

THE CURSE OF KING TUT

An ancient Egyptian relic with a strange inscription had an honored place in the spacious London apartment of Lord Westbury for seven years. It had been taken from the tomb of the boy Pharaoh King Tutankhamen by Howard Carter, the famous English archaeologist who had discovered and excavated the tomb. The inscription as translated by scholars read:

DEATH SHALL COME ON SWIFT WINGS
TO WHO TOUCHETH THE TOMB
OF THE PHARAOHS.

(Above quoted from *The Desperate Years* by James D. Horan, Bonanza Books, New York, page 22.)

This is the famous curse of King Tut and 14 people connected with the opening of the tomb died in violent or mysterious circumstances over as many years. One died in Egypt from an infected mosquito bite. Another was killed in a car crash near Columbus Texas.

Lord Westbury made little of the curse. 'Nothing to it' he told reporters. 'Just a lot of superstition.'

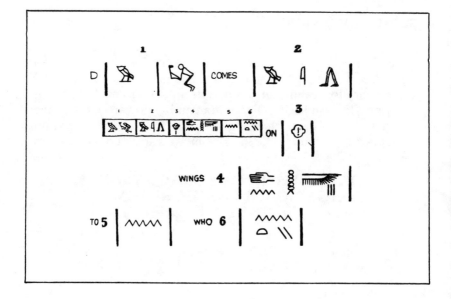

Then one day in 1930 he stepped out of a seventh-floor window of his London apartment. As Westbury's body was being taken to a crematorium the hearse knocked down and killed an 8-year-old boy.

Notice that the death glyph is a man splitting his own head with an axe. Recall a time when you painfully bit your inner lip. Recall a time when you hit your shins against a chair or table or stool in a dark room. Recall a time when a cigarette stuck to your lip and your fingers slid up the cigarette resulting in painful burn and shower of sparks. Death is here conceived as coming from within, as an implanted self-destruct mechanism. A curse operates very much like a virus and is equally indiscriminate. Notice that the glyph for who is bread and water. A curse is a formula and any who can be fitted into this formula by association ... bread and water diet, bread lines, money, since bread is an old slang term for money, Watergate, floods, tidal waves, wet streets ...

Written across a dark sky in silver letters ... THE 1930s.

Cut to end of excavated passage ... 'This is it gentlemen. The tomb of Tutankhamen.'

Glyphs blow out across the dust bowl. Bank robbers shoot it out with FBI agents.

Strikes, bread lines, ruined brokers leaping from windows.

Luxurious London apartment of Lord Westbury. Westbury is drunk. The lights go out. He reels to his feet shouting 'GRIMSY ... BRING CANDLES ... OPEN THE CURTAINS ... Nipped off to the pub most likely' ... He gets up to open the curtains and stumbles over a coffee table ... crash of glass ... his body draped in a red curtain plummets to the street ...

Lord Westbury's coffin covered with flowers is put into hearse by pall bearers ... gangster funerals intercut ...

Hearse on way to crematorium. Driver is smoking cigarette. He puts two fingers on cigarette to remove after inhale. Cigarette sticks to his lip. Finger slides up cigarette burning fingers and showering his pants with sparks. Driver curses brushing sparks off pants. He looks up and slams on the brakes. Hearse skids on wet street.

Casket jolts violently forward.

Eight-Year-Old Boy Dead on Westbury Street.

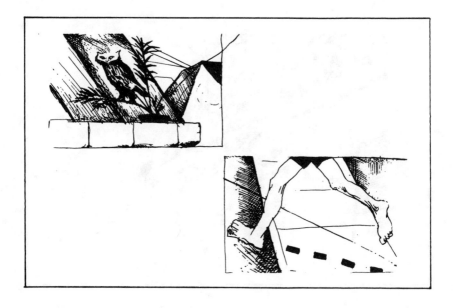

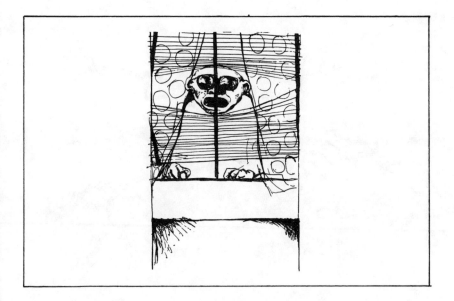

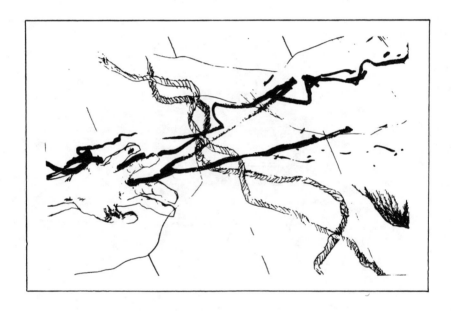

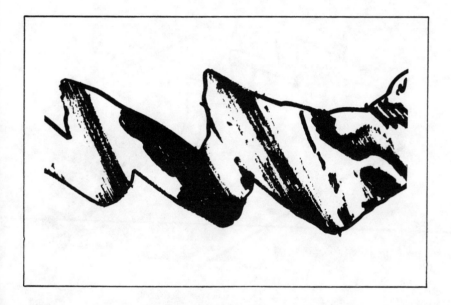

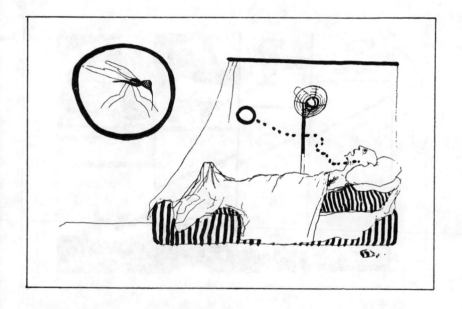

DEATH   IN THE PRESENCE OF   BY MEANS OF
                    ALAMOUT

Hassan i Sabbah was a boyhood friend of poet Omar Kyam.
He became a convert to the dissident Ishmaelian sect and fled
from his native Persia to Egypt where he spent several years. I
put a question to CONTROL:

Question: What secret did Hassan i Sabbah learn in Egypt
that enabled him to control and activate his assassins from a
distance?

Answer: Energy from virus.

After years of wandering with a handful of followers Hassan i
Sabbah established himself in the mountain fortress of
Alamout in what is now northern Iran. Dispatching his
assassins from this fortress he became known as the Old Man
of the Mountain, Master of the Assassins. What training did
his assassins undergo? We know that Alamout was an all male
community of several hundred apprentice assassins.
Undoubtedly homosexual practices formed a part of the
training which sometimes lasted for years. His assassins
spread terror through the Moslem world. Whenever a move
was planned against Alamout the assassins struck. Energy
from virus? And what is a virus? Perhaps simply a pictorial
series like Egyptian glyphs that *makes itself real*. Before the

Death   In The Presence of By Means of ALAMOUT

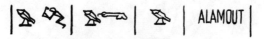

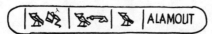

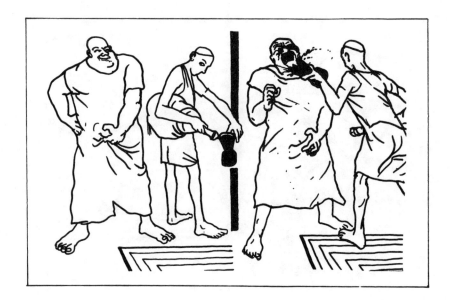

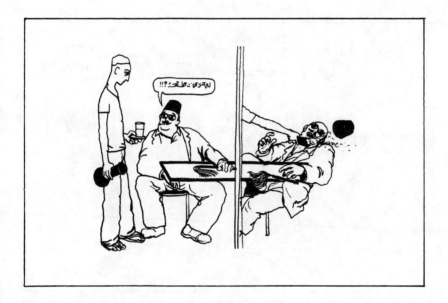

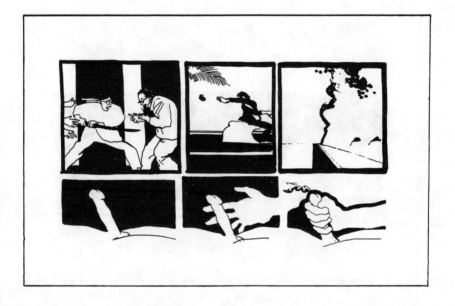

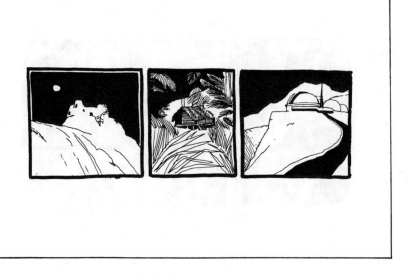

pictures conceived in opposition to Alamout could make themselves real the assassins struck, deriving their energy precisely from these hostile pictures. A general who planned an expedition against Alamout was killed by an old man who had worked in his garden for ten years. Caliphs, Sultans, Emirs were killed in their palaces by trusted servants.

Brion Gysin has just returned from a trip to the fortress of Alamout in northern Iran. He showed me photos of the ruins and a copy of an article he had written on Hassan i Sabbah the Old Man of the Mountain and his assassins. The information assembled in this article raises a number of questions.

The living quarters are quite small and it seems that not more than forty people could have lived there at one time. Certainly the historical estimates of several hundred resident assassins must be modified. Emphasis was on inaccessibility. Altitude of the living quarters is about ten thousand feet. The fortress must have been bitterly cold in winter. There is very little timber in this area and what fuel they had available must have been used for cooking. We must conclude that Alamout was virtually without heat during the long cold winters ...?

The word assassin derives from hashiesh. It is reported that the Old Man gave his followers hashiesh which transported them to a garden of delights. They were then told they could live in the garden forever after carrying out an assignment of assassination. Those who have used hashiesh will question this legend. The effects of hashiesh alone under ordinary circumstances will hardly produce convincing hallucinations of paradise ...?

There are persistent reports of an extensive library at Alamout that finally fell into the hands of the Mongols. However no texts that can reliably be traced to Alamout have come to light. Of what then did these books consist? Why and how have they remained unavailable to scholars?

In a number of discussions we arrived at some possible answers to these perplexing questions:

Question: How do you sit out a freezing winter at ten thousand feet with no heat?

Answer: Opium.

Question: Under what circumstances could hashiesh produce the hallucinating effects that would account for the legend of the garden?

Answer: During opium withdrawal.

Question: How else do you sit out such a winter?

Answer: You don't sit. You work all day. At night you have sufficient cover to prevent fatal refrigeration.

Question: Under what other circumstances could hashiesh produce the effects described in the legend?

Answer: After the privations of such a winter.

Question: How else could you beat the cold?

Answer: Take a tip from the Siberian Chuckchee: Construct a wood frame about two feet high, eight feet wide and long enough to accommodate personnel. Cover frame with leather or rugs to form a long shallow box. All hands strip naked and get in the box heating it with their bodies. This promotes esprit de corps.

Three systems here described would be more effective if used in rotation.

Question: Of what did the missing books consist?

Answer: Hassan i Sabbah spent several years in Egypt during which he seems to have picked up some clue that subsequently enabled him to train and control his assassins. This clue may have been Egyptian hieroglyphs and the missing books may have consisted of text and extended glyphs similar to this Book of Breathings: pictures of the students in training, the fortress, the garden; detailed illustrated blue-prints for operations against enemy personnel. This means that some students were trained as scribes.

Question: Why have none of these books come to light?

Answer: Too hot to handle. They were destroyed or kept secret. Similar methods now used by CIA and other intelligence agencies: to produce assassinations and revolutions: the operation is mapped out in stills animation and moving film.

CIA man looks through a stack of photos and picks one.

'Now that's a nice face for you ... good strong lines ... cast him as the Strong Man who will bring law and order peace and prosperity back to Chile. He'll win an Oscar for the ugliest performance of the year ...'

This operation applies the curse formula. Recall that the death glyph is a man splitting his head with an axe. To what forms of self-destructive behaviour is the target liable? Is he a fast reckless driver? Smoke too much? Eat too much? Drunk

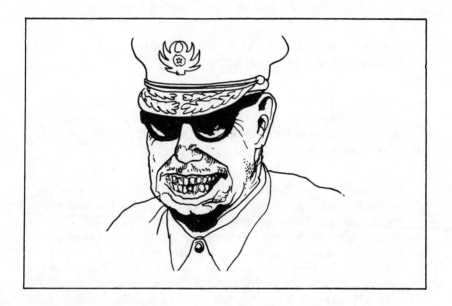

too often? Prone to loss of temper or other emotional excesses? Alternative programs can be set up and the operation computerized.

Newsweek, October 1, 1973, page 8 ... 'Allende knew he was on the verge of being ousted ... took to drinking heavily ... tension getting the better of him ... at one meeting he broke down and wept uncontrollably and had to be led away ...'

A curse is activated by hate. Mixture of sexual and hostile elements in the basic death formula.

Newsweek, October 1, 1973, page 8 ... 'Railing against the moral decadence of the Allende government and spreading lurid rumors of a secret Presidential cache of pornographic films and sex devices ...'

To control any situation it is simply necessary to place yourself and keep yourself in Third Terminal Position with respect to other participants in the situation. T.T.P. is no-effect position. Hassan i Sabbah took and held Alamout, a Third Terminal from which he could reach and affect his enemies and where they could not reach or affect him. This is a classic 3T and shows how simple the operation is. The Old Man has taken up 3T in Alamout. Let us see where this places him with regard to his opponents.

Terminal 1: General Whoever. The Old Man has his picture in his books. He knows the General's weaknesses and fears. The General knows nothing about The Old Man.

Terminal 2: Anyone with whom the good and soon to be lamented General comes *into direct contact* ... servants, friends, associates and above all *sexual partners*.

Terminal 3: Anything the General cannot control or affect but which can control and affect him: in this case *Alamout*. If the General can't get it up or if he has indigestion he will attribute this to Alamout.

He who controls the Third Terminal controls T1 and T2 as well. The Old Man knows a lot about the General. The General doesn't know anything about him. A servant who will kill the General will be accepted into his service. It is written in the books. Destructive sexual partners will be welcomed. The Old Man knows every kink of the General. *3T cone taken and held sucks in everything in the General's psyche and environment that he cannot understand or control so that he understands and controls less and less.*

Now of course The Old Man could plant someone in the General's kitchen to hex his hard ons or give him the shits but he doesn't really need to do that. The General knows that *he can do that* and that is enough to hex his hard on and give him the shits and make him fire a kitchen full of loyal servants leaving the way open for The Old Man's agents.

Possession of the Books puts The Old Man in 3T.P. He has his opponents in his books. They do not have the information access or skill to compile such books on him. The Old Man must have been a very great artist.

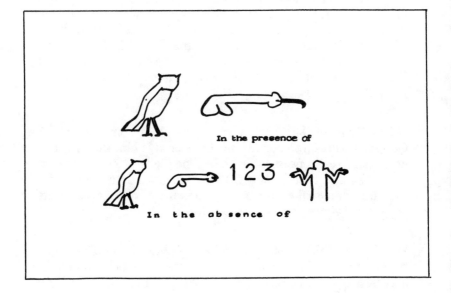

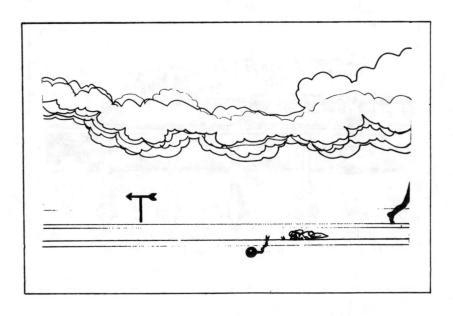

ELECTRONIC REVOLUTION

In 'The Invisible Generation' first published in *IT* and in the *Los Angeles Free Press* in 1966, I consider the potential of thousands of people with recorders, portable and stationary, messages passed along like signal drums, a parody of the President's speech up and down the balconies, in and out open windows, through walls, over courtyards, taken up by barking dogs, muttering bums, music, traffic down windy streets, across parks and soccer fields. Illusion is a revolutionary weapon. To point out some specific uses of prerecorded cut/up tapes played back in the streets as a revolutionary weapon:

To spread rumors

Put ten operators with carefully prepared recordings out at the rush hour and see how quick the words get around. People don't know where they heard it but they heard it.

To discredit opponents

Take a recorded Wallace speech, cut in stammering coughs sneezes hiccoughs snarls pain screams fear whimperings apoplectic sputterings slobbering drooling idiot noises sex and animal sound effects and play it back in the streets subways stations parks political rallies.

As a front line weapon to produce and escalate riots

There is nothing mystical about this operation. Riot sound

effects can produce an actual riot in a riot situation. *Recorded police whistles will draw cops. Recorded gunshots, and their guns are out.*

'MY GOD, THEY'RE KILLING US.'

A guardsman said later: 'I heard the shots and saw my buddy go down, his face covered in blood (turned out he'd been hit by a stone from a sling shot) and I thought, well this is it.' BLOODY WEDNESDAY. A DAZED AMERICA COUNTED 23 DEAD AND 32 WOUNDED, 6 CRITICALLY.

Here is a run-of-the-mill, pre-riot situation. Protestors have been urged to demonstrate peacefully, police and guardsmen to exercise restraint. Ten tape recorders strapped under their coats, play back and record controlled from lapel buttons. They have prerecorded riot sound effects from Chicago, Paris, Mexico City, Kent, Ohio. If they adjust sound level of recordings to surrounding sound levels, they will not be detected. Police scuffle with the demonstrators. The operators converge. Turn on Chicago record, play back, move on to the next scuffles, record, play back, keep moving. Things are hotting up, a cop is down groaning. Shrill chorus of recorded pig squeals and parody groans.

Could you cool a riot recording the calmest cop and the most reasonable demonstrators? Maybe! However, it's a lot easier to start trouble than stop it. Just pointing out that cut/ups on the tape recorder can be used as a weapon. You'll observe that the operators are making a cut/up as they go. They are cutting in Chicago, Paris, Mexico City, Kent, Ohio with the present sound effects at random, and that is a cut/up.

As a long-range weapon to scramble and nullify associational lines put down by mass media

The control of the mass media depends on laying down lines of association. When the lines are cut the associational connections are broken.

President Johnson burst into a swank apartment, held three

maids at gunpoint, 26 miles north of Saigon yesterday.

You can cut the mutter line of the mass media and put the altered mutter line out in the streets with a tape recorder. Consider the mutter line of the daily press. It goes up with the morning papers, millions of people reading the same words, belching chewing swearing chuckling reacting to the same words. In different ways, of course. A motion praising Mr. Callaghan's action in banning the South African Cricket Tour has spoiled the colonel's breakfast. All reacting one way or another to the paper world of unseen events which becomes an integral part of your reality. You will notice that this process is continually subject to random juxtaposition. Just what sign did you see in the Green Park station as you glanced up from the *People?* Just who called as you were reading your letter in the *Times?* What were you reading when your wife broke a dish in the kitchen? An unreal paper world and yet completely real because it is actually happening. Mutter line of the *Evening News,* TV. Fix yourself on millions of people all watching Jesse James or the Virginian at the same time. International mutter line of the weekly news magazine always dated a week ahead. Have you noticed it's the kiss of death to be on the front cover of *Time.* Madam Nhu was there when her husband was killed and her government fell. Verwoerd was on the front cover of *Time* when a demon tapeworm gave the order for his death through a messenger of the same. Read the Bible, kept to himself, no bad habits, you know the type. Old reliable, read all about it.

So stir in news stories, TV plays, stock market quotations, adverts and put the altered mutter line out in the streets.

The underground press serves as the only effective counter to a growing power and more sophisticated techniques used by establishment mass media to falsify, misrepresent, misquote, rule out of consideration as *a priori* ridiculous or simply ignore and blot out of existence: data, books, discoveries that they consider prejudicial to establishment interest.

I suggest that the underground press could perform this function much more effectively by the use of cut/up techniques. For example, prepare cut/ups of the ugliest reactionary statements you can find and surround them with the ugliest pictures. Now give it the drool, slobber, animal-noise treatment and put it out on the mutter line with recorders. Run a scramble page in every issue of a transcribed tape-recorded cut/up of news, radio, and TV. Put the recordings out on the mutter line before the paper hits the stand. It gives you a funny feeling to see a headline that's been going round and round in your head. The underground press could add a mutter line to their adverts and provide a unique advertising service. Cut the product in with pop tunes, cut the product in with advertising slogans and jingles of other products and syphon off the sales. Anybody who doubts that these techniques work has only to put them to the test. The techniques here described are in use by the CIA and agents of other countries. Ten years ago they were making systematic street recordings in every district of Paris. I recall the Voice of America man in Tangier and a room full of tape recorders and you could hear some strange sounds through the wall. Kept to himself, hello in the hall. Nobody was ever allowed in that room, not even a fatima. Of course, there are many technical elaborations like long-range directional mikes. When cutting the prayer call in with hog grunts it doesn't pay to be walking around the market place with a portable tape recorder.

An article in *New Scientist* June 4, 1970, page 470, entitled 'Electronic Arts of Noncommunication' by Richard C. French gives the clue for more precise technical instructions.

In 1968, with the help of Ian Sommerville and Anthony Balch, I took a short passage of my recorded voice and cut it into intervals of one twenty-fourth of a second on movie tape – (movie tape is larger and easier to splice) – and rearranged the order of the 24th-second intervals of recorded speech. The original words are quite unintelligible but new words emerge. The voice is still there and you can immediately recognize the speaker. Also the tone of voice remains. If the tone is friendly, hostile, sexual, poetic, sarcastic, lifeless, despairing, this will be apparent in the altered sequence.

I did not realize at the time that I was using a technique that has been in existence since 1881 ... I quote from Mr. French's article ... 'Designs for speech scramblers go back to 1881 and the desire to make telephone and radio communications unintelligible to third parties has been with us ever since' ... The message is scrambled in transmission and then unscrambled at the other end. There are many of these speech scrambling devices that work on different principles ... 'Another device which saw service during the war was the time division scrambler. The signal is chopped up into elements .005 cm long. These elements are taken in groups or frames and rearranged in a new sequence. Imagine that the speech recorded is recorded on magnetic tape which is cut into pieces 2 cm long and the pieces rearranged into a new sequence. This can actually be done and gives a good idea what speech sounds like when scrambled in this way.'

This I had done in 1968. And this is an extension of the cut/up method. The simplest cut/up cuts a page down the middle into four sections. Section 1 is then placed with section 4 and section 3 with section 2 in a new sequence. Carried further we can break the page down into smaller and smaller units in altered sequences.

The original purpose of scrambling devices was to make the message unintelligible without the unscrambling code. Another use for speech scramblers could be to impose thought control on a mass scale. Consider the human body and nervous system as unscrambling devices. A common virus like the cold sore could sensitize the subject to unscramble messages. Drugs like LSD and Dim-N could also act as unscrambling devices. Moreover, the mass media could sensitize millions of people to receive scrambled versions of the same set of data. Remember that when the human nervous system unscrambles a scrambled message this will seem to the subject like his very own ideas which just occurred to him, which indeed it did.

Take a card, any card. In most cases he will not suspect its extraneous origin. That is the run-of-the-mill newspaper reader who receives the scrambled message uncritically and assumes that it reflects his own opinions independently arrived at. On the other hand, the subject may recognize or suspect the extraneous origin of voices that are literally hatching out in his head. Then we have the classic syndrome of paranoid psychosis. Subject hears voices. Anyone can be made to hear voices with scrambling techniques. It is not difficult to expose him to the actual scrambled message, any part of which can be made intelligible. This can be done with street recorders, recorders in cars, doctored radio and TV sets. In his own flat if possible, if not in some bar or restaurant he frequents. If he doesn't talk to himself, he soon will do. You bug his flat. Now he is really round the bend hearing his own voice out of radio and TV broadcasts and the conversation of passing strangers. See how easy it is? Remember the scrambled message is partially unintelligible and in any case he gets the tone. Hostile white voices unscrambled by a Negro will also activate by association every occasion on which he has been threatened or humiliated by whites. To carry it further you can use recordings of voices known to him. You can turn him against his friends by hostile scrambled messages in a friend's voice. This will activate all his disagreements with that friend. You can condition him to like his enemies by friendly scrambled messages in enemy voices.

On the other hand the voices can be friendly and reassuring. He is now working for the CIA, the GPU, or whatever, and these are his orders. They now have an agent who has no information to give away and who doesn't have to be paid. And he is now completely under control. If he doesn't obey orders they can give him the hostile voice treatment. No, 'They' are not God or super technicians from outer space. Just technicians operating with well-known equipment and using techniques that can be duplicated by anybody else who can buy and operate this equipment.

To see how scrambling techniques could work on a mass media scale, imagine that a news magazine like *Time* got out a whole issue a week before publication and filled it with news based on predictions following a certain line, without attempting the impossible, giving our boys a boost in every story and the Commies as many defeats and casualties as possible, a whole issue of *Time* formed from slanted prediction of future news. Now imagine this scrambled out through the mass media.

With minimal equipment you can do the same thing on a smaller scale. You need a scrambling device, TV, radio, two video cameras, a ham radio station and a simple photo studio with a few props and actors. For a start you scramble the news all together and spit it out every which way on ham radio and street recorders. You construct fake news broadcasts on video camera. For the pictures you can use mostly old footage. Mexico City will do for a riot in Saigon and vice versa. For a riot in Santiago, Chile you can use the Londonderry pictures. Nobody knows the difference. Fires, earthquakes, plane crashes can be moved around. For example, here is a plane crash, 112 dead north of Barcelona and here is a plane crash in Toronto 108 dead. So move the picture of the Barcelona plane crash over to Toronto and Toronto to Barcelona. And you scramble your fabricated news in with actual news broadcasts.

You have an advantage which your opposing player does not have. He must conceal his manipulations. You are under no such necessity. In fact you can advertise the fact that you are writing news in advance and trying to make it happen by techniques which anybody can use. And that makes you NEWS. And a TV personality as well, if you play it right. You want the widest possible circulation for your cut/up video tapes. Cut/up techniques could swamp the mass media with total illusion.

Fictional dailies retroactively cancelled the San Francisco earthquake and the Halifax explosion as journalistic hoaxes, and doubt released from the skin law extendable and ravenous, consumed all the facts of history.

Mr. French concludes his article ... 'The use of modern microelectric integrated circuits could lower the cost of speech scramblers enough to see them in use by private citizens. Codes and ciphers have always had a strong appeal to most people and I think scramblers will as well ...'

It is generally assumed that speech must be consciously understood to cause an effect. Early experiments with subliminal images have shown that this is not true. A number of research projects could be based on speech scramblers. We have all seen the experiment where someone speaking hears his own recorded voice back a few seconds later. Soon he cannot go on talking. Would scrambled speech have the same effect? To what extent are scrambled messages actually unscrambled by experimental subjects? To what extent does a language act as an unscrambling device, western languages tending to unscramble in either-or conflict terms? To what extent does the tone of voice used by a speaker impose a certain unscrambling sequence on the listener?

Many of the cut/up tapes would be entertaining and in fact entertainment is the most promising field for cut/up techniques. Imagine a pop festival like Phun City scheduled for July 24th, 25th, 26th, 1970 at Ecclesden Common, Patching, near Worthing, Sussex. Festival area comprised of car park and camping area, a rock auditorium, a village with booths and cinema, a large wooded area. A number of tape recorders are planted in the woods and the village. As many as possible so as to lay down a grid of sound over the whole festival. Recorders have tapes of prerecorded material, music, news broadcasts, recordings from other festivals, etc. At all times some of the recorders are playing back and some are recording. The recorders recording at any time are of course recording the crowd and the other tape recorders that are playing back at varying distances. This cuts in the crowd who will be hearing their own voices back. Playback, windback and record could be electronically controlled with varying intervals. Or they could be hand operated, the operator deciding what intervals of playback, record, and windback to use. Effect is greatly increased by a large number of festival goers with portable recorders playing back and recording as they walk around the festival. We can carry it further with projection screens and video cameras. Some of the material projected is pre-prepared, sex films, films of other festivals, and this material is cut in with live TV broadcasts and shots of the crowd. Of course, the rock festival will be cut in on the screens, thousands of fans with portable recorders recording and playing back, the singer could direct playback and record. Set up an area for travelling performers, jugglers, animal acts, snake charmers, singers, musicians, and cut these acts in. Film and tape from the festival, edited for the best material, could then be used at other festivals.

Quite a lot of equipment and engineering to set it up. The festival could certainly be enhanced if as many festival-goers as possible bring portable tape recorders to record and play back at the festival.

Any message, music, conversation you want to pass around, bring it pre-recorded on tape so everybody takes pieces of your tape home.

Research project: to find out to what extent scrambled messages are unscrambled, that is, scanned out by experimental subjects. The simplest experiment consists in playing back a scrambled message to subject. Message could contain simple commands. Does the scrambled message have any command value comparable to post-hypnotic suggestion? Is the actual content of the message received? What drugs, if any, increase ability to unscramble messages? Do subjects vary widely in this ability? Are scrambled messages in the subject's own voice more effective than messages in other voices? Are messages scrambled in certain voices more easily unscrambled by specific subjects? Is the message more potent with both word and image scrambled on video tape? Now to use, for example, a videotape message with a unified emotional content. Let us say the message is fear. For this we take all the past fear shots of the subject we can collect or evoke. We cut these in with fear words and pictures, with threats, etc. This is all acted out and would be upsetting enough in any case. Now let's try it scrambled and see if we get an even stronger effect. The subject's blood pressure, rate of heart beat, and brain waves are recorded as we play back the scrambled tape. His face is photographed and visible to him on video camera at all times. The actual scrambling of the tape can be done in two ways. It can be a completely random operation like pulling pieces out of a hat and if this is done several consecutive units may occur together, yielding an identifiable picture or intelligible word. Both methods of course can be used at varying intervals. Blood pressure, heart beat, and brain-wave recordings will show the operator what material is producing the strongest reaction, and he will of course zero in. And remember that the subject can see his face at all times and his face is being photographed. As the Peeping Tom said, the most frightening thing is fear in your own face. If the subject becomes too disturbed we have peace and safety tapes ready.

Now here is a sex tape: this consists of a sex scene acted out by the ideal sexual object of the subject and his ideal self image. Shown straight it might be exciting enough, now scramble it. It takes a few seconds for scrambled tapes to hatch out, and then? Can scrambled sex tapes zeroing in on the subject's reactions and brain waves result in spontaneous orgasm? Can this be extended to other functions of the body? A mike secreted in the water closet and all his shits and farts recorded and scrambled in with stern nanny voices commanding him to shit, and the young liberal shits in his pants on the platform right under Old Glory. Could laugh tapes, sneeze tapes, hiccough tapes, cough tapes, give rise to laughing, sneezing, hiccoughing, and coughing?

To what extent can physical illness be induced by scrambled illness tapes? Take, for example, a sound and color picture of a subject with a cold. Later, when subject is fully recovered, we take color and sound film of recovered subject. We now scramble the cold pictures and sound track in with present sound and image track. We also project the cold pictures on present pictures. Now we try using some of Mr. Hubbard's reactive mind phrases which are supposed in themselves to produce illness. To be me, to be you, to stay here, to stay there, to be a body, to be bodies, to stay present, to stay past. Now we scramble all this in together and show it to the subject. Could seeing and hearing this sound and image track, scrambled down to very small units, bring about an attack of cold virus? If such a cold tape does actually produce an attack of cold virus we cannot say that we have created a virus, perhaps we have merely activated a latent virus. Many viruses, as you know, are latent in the body and may be activated. We can try the same with cold sore, with hepatitis, always remembering that we may be activating a latent virus

and in no sense creating a laboratory virus. However, we may
be in a position to do this. Is a virus perhaps simply very small
units of sound and image? Remember the only image a virus
has is the image and sound track it can impose on you. The
yellow eyes of jaundice, the pustules of smallpox, etc. imposed
on you against your will. The same is certainly true of
scrambled word and image, its existence is the word and
image it can make you unscramble. Take a card, any card.
This does not mean that it is actually a virus. Perhaps to
construct a laboratory virus we would need both camera and
sound crew and a biochemist as well. I quote from the
International Paris Tribune an article on the synthetic gene: 'Dr.
Har Gobind Khorana has made a gene-synthetic.'

'It is the beginning of the end,' this was the immediate
reaction to this news from the science attaché at one of
Washington's major embassies. 'If you can make genes you
can eventually make new viruses for which there are no cures.
Any little country with good biochemists could make such
biological weapons. It would take only a small laboratory. If it
can be done, somebody will do it.' For example, a death virus
could be created that carries the coded message of death. A
death tape, in fact. No doubt the technical details are complex
and perhaps a team of sound and camera men working with
biochemists would gives us the answer.

And now the question as to whether scrambling techniques
could be used to spread helpful and pleasant messages.
Perhaps. On the other hand, the scrambled words and tape
act like a virus in that they force something on the subject
against his will. More to the point would be to discover how
the old scanning patterns could be altered so that the subject
liberates his own spontaneous scanning pattern.

New Scientist, July 2, 1970 ... Current memory theory posits
a seven second temporary 'buffer store' preceding the main
one: a blow on the head wipes out memory of this much prior
time because it erases the contents of the buffer. Daedalus
observes that the sense of the present also covers just this
range and so suggests that our sensory input is in effect
recorded on an endless time loop, providing some seven

seconds of delay for scanning before erasure. In this time the brain edits, makes sense of, and selects for storage key features. The weird *déjà vu* sensation that 'now' has happened before is clearly due to brief erasure failure, so that we encounter already stored memory data coming round again. Time dragging or racing must reflect tape speed. A simple experiment will demonstrate this erasure process in operation. Making street recordings and playing them back, you will hear things you do not remember, sometimes said in a loud clear voice, must have been quite close to you, nor do you necessarily remember them when you hear the recording back. The sound has been erased according to a scanning pattern which is automatic. This means that what you notice and store as memory as you walk down a street is scanned out of a much larger selection of data which is then erased from the memory. For the walker the signs he passed, people he has passed, are erased from his mind and cease to exist for him. Now to make this scanning process conscious and controllable, try this:

Walk down a city block with a camera and take what you notice, moving the camera around as closely as possible to follow the direction of your eyes. The point is to make the camera your eyes and take what your eyes are scanning out of the larger picture. At the same time take the street at wide angle from a series of still positions. The street of the operator is, of course, the street as seen by the operator. It is different from the street seen at wide angle. Much of it is in fact missing. Now you can make arbitrary scanning patterns – that is cover first one side of the street and then the other in accordance with a preconceived plan. So you are breaking down the automatic scanning patterns. You could also make color scanning patterns, that is, scan out green, blue, red, etc. insofar as you can with your camera. That is, you are using an arbitrary preconceived scanning pattern, in order to break down automatic scanning patterns. A number of operators do this and then scramble in their takes together and with wide angle takes. This could train the subject to see at a wider angle and also to ignore and erase at will.

Now, all this is readily subject to experimental verification
on control subjects. Nor need the equipment be all that
complicated. I have shown how it could work with feedback
from brain waves and visceral response and videotape photos
of subject taken while he is seeing and hearing the tape,
simply to show optimum effectiveness. You can start with two
tape recorders. The simplest scrambling device is scissors and
splicing equipment. You can start scrambling words, make
any kind of tapes and scramble them and observe the effects
on friends and on yourself. Next step is sound film and then
video camera. Of course results from individual experiments
could lead to mass experiments, mass fear tapes, riot tapes,
etc. The possibilities here for research and experiment are
virtually unlimited and I have simply made a few very simple
suggestions.

'A virus is characterised and limited by obligate cellular
parasitism. All viruses must parasitise living cells for their
replication. For all viruses the infection cycle comprises entry
into the host, intracellular replication, and escape from the
body of the host to initiate a new cycle in a fresh host.' I am
quoting here from *Mechanisms of Virus Infection* edited by Dr.
Wilson Smith. In its wild state the virus has not proved to be a
very adaptable organism. Some viruses have burned
themselves out since they were 100 percent fatal and there
were no reservoirs. Each strain of virus is rigidly programmed
for a certain attack on certain tissues. If the attack fails, the
virus does not gain a new host. There are, of course, virus
mutations, and the influenza virus has proved quite versatile
in this way. Generally it's the simple repetition of the same
method of entry, and if that method is blocked by any body or
other agency such as interferon, the attack fails. By and large,
our virus is a stupid organism. Now we can think for the virus,
devise a number of alternate methods of entry. For example,
the host is simultaneously attacked by an ally virus who tells
him that everything is alright and by a pain and fear virus. So
the virus is now using an old method of entry, namely, the
tough cop and the con cop.

We have considered the possibility that a virus can be

activated or even created by very small units of sound and image. So conceived, the virus can be made to order in the laboratory. Ah, but for the takes to be effective, you must have also the actual virus and what is this so actual virus? New viruses turn up from time to time but from where do they turn up? Well, let's see how we could make a virus turn up. We plot now our virus's symptoms and make a scramble tape. The most susceptible subjects, that is those who reproduce some of the desired symptoms, will then be scrambled into more tapes till we scramble our virus into existence. This birth of a virus occurs when our virus is able to reproduce itself in a host and pass itself on to another host. Perhaps, too, with the virus under laboratory control it can be tamed for useful purposes. Imagine, for example, a sex virus. It so inflames the sex centers in the back brain that the host is driven mad from sexuality, all other considerations are blacked out. Parks full of naked, frenzied people, shitting, pissing, ejaculating, and screaming. So the virus could be malignant, blacking out all regulation and end in exhaustion, convulsions, and death.

Now let us attempt the same thing with tape. We organize a sex-tape festival. 100,000 people bring their scrambled sex tapes, and video tapes as well, to scramble in together. Projected on vast screens, muttering out over the crowd, sometimes it slows down so you see a few seconds, then scrambled again, then slow down, scramble. Soon it will scramble them all naked. The cops and the National Guard are stripping down. LET'S GET OURSELVES SOME CIVVIES. Now a thing like that could be messy, but those who survive it recover from the madness. Or, say, a small select group of really like-minded people get together with their sex tapes, you see the process is now being brought under control. And the fact that anybody can do it is in itself a limiting factor.

Here is Mr. Hart, who wants to infect everyone with his own image and turn them all into himself, so he scrambles himself and dumps himself out in search of worthy vessels. If nobody else knows about scrambling techniques he might scramble himself quite a stable of replicas. But anybody can do it. So go on, scramble your sex words out, and find suitable mates.

If you want to, scramble yourself out there, every stale joke, fart, chew, sneeze, and stomach rumble. If your trick no work you better run. Everybody doing it, they all scramble in together and the populations of the earth just settle down a nice even brown color. Scrambles is the democratic way, the way of full cellular representation. Scrambles is the American way.

I have suggested that virus can be created to order in the laboratory from very small units of sound and image. Such a preparation is not in itself biologically active but it could activate or even create virus in susceptible subjects. A carefully prepared jaundice tape could activate or create the jaundice virus in liver cells, especially in cases where the liver is already damaged. The operator is in effect directing a virus revolution of the cells. Since DOR seems to attack those exposed to it at the weakest point, release of this force could coincide with virus attack. Reactive mind phrases could serve the same purpose of rendering subjects more susceptible to virus attack.

It will be seen that scrambled speech already has many of the characteristics of virus. When the speech takes and unscrambles, this occurs compulsively and against the will of the subject. A virus must remind you of its presence. Whether it is the nag of a cold sore or the torturing spasms of rabies the virus reminds you of its unwanted presence. 'HERE ME IS.'

So does scrambled word and image. The units are unscrambling compulsively, presenting certain words and images to the subject and this repetitive presentation is irritating certain bodily and neural areas. The cells so irritated can produce over a period of time the biologic virus units. We now have a new virus that can be communicated and indeed the subject may be desperate to communicate this thing that is bursting inside him. He is heavy with the load. Could this load be good and beautiful? Is it possible to create a virus which will communicate calm and sweet reasonableness? A virus must parasitise a host in order to survive. It uses the cellular material of the host to make copies of itself. In most cases this is damaging to the host. The virus gains entrance by fraud and maintains itself by force. An unwanted guest who makes you sick to look at is never good or beautiful. It is moreover a guest who always repeats itself word for word take for take.

Remember the life cycle of a virus ... penetration of a cell or activation within the cell, replication within the cell, escape from cell to invade other cells, escape from host to infect a new host. This infection can take place in many ways and those who find themselves heavy with the load of a new virus generally use a shotgun technique to cover a wide range of infection routes ... cough, sneeze, spit and fart at every opportunity. Save shit, piss, snot, scabs, sweat-stained clothes and all bodily secretions for dehydration. The composite dust can be unobtrusively billowed out a roach bellows in subways, dropped from windows in bags, or sprayed out a crop duster ... Carry with you at all times an assortment of vectors ... lice, fleas, bed bugs, and little aviaries of mosquitoes and biting flies filled with your blood ... I see no beauty in that.

There is only one case of a favorable virus influence benefiting an obscure species of Australian mice. On the other hand, if a virus produces no damaging symptoms we have no way of ascertaining its existence and this happens with latent virus infections. It has been suggested that yellow races resulted from a jaundice-like virus which produced a permanent mutation not necessarily damaging, which was passed along genetically. The same may be true of the word. The word itself may be a virus that has achieved a permanent status with the host. However, no known virus in existence at the present time acts in this manner, so the question of a beneficent virus remains open. It seems advisable to concentrate on a general defense against all virus.

Ron Hubbard, founder of scientology, says that certain words and word combinations can produce serious illnesses and mental disturbances. I can claim some skill in the scrivener's trade, but I cannot guarantee to write a passage that will make someone physically ill. If Mr. Hubbard's claim is justified, this is certainly a matter for further research, and we can easily find out experimentally whether his claim is justified or not. Mr. Hubbard bases the power he attributes to words on his theory of engrams. An engram is defined as word, sound, image recorded by the subject in a period of pain and unconsciousness. Some of this material may be reassuring: 'I think he's going to be alright.' Reassuring material is an ally engram. Ally engrams, according to Mr. Hubbard, are just as bad as hostile pain engrams. Any part of this recording played back to the subject later will reactivate operation pain, he may actually develop a headache and feel depressed, anxious, or tense. Well, Mr. Hubbard's engram theory is very easily subject to experimental verification. Take ten volunteer subjects, subject them to a pain stimulus accompanied by certain words and sounds and images. You can act out little skits.

'Quickly, nurse, before I lose my little nigger,' bellows the southern surgeon, and now a beefy white hand falls on the fragile black shoulder. 'Yes, he's going to be alright. He's going to pull through.'

'If I had my way I'd let these animals die on the operating table.'

'You do not have your way, you have your duty as a doctor, we must do everything in our power to save human lives.'

And so forth.

It is the tough cop and the con cop. The ally engram is ineffective without the pain engram, just as the con cop's arm around your shoulder, his soft persuasive voice in your ear, are indeed sweet nothings without the tough cop's blackjack. Now to what extent can words recorded during medical unconsciousness be recalled during hypnosis or scientological processing? To what extent does the playback of this material affect the subject unpleasantly? Is the effect enhanced by scrambling the material, pain and ally, at very short intervals? It would seem that a scrambled engram's picture could almost dump an operating scene right in the subject's lap. Mr. Hubbard has charted his version of what he calls the reactive mind. This is roughly similar to Freud's *id*, a sort of built-in self-defeating mechanism. As set forth by Mr. Hubbard this consists of a number of quite ordinary phrases. He claims that reading these phrases, or hearing them spoken, can cause illness, and gives this as his reason for not publishing this material. Is he perhaps saying that these are magic words? Spells, in fact? If so they could be quite a weapon scrambled up with imaginative sound-and-image track. Here now is the magic that turns men into swine. To be an animal: a lone pig grunts, shits, squeals and slobbers down garbage. To be animals: a chorus of a thousand pigs. Cut that in with video-tape police pictures and play it back to them and see if you get a reaction from this so reactive mind.

Now here is another. To be a body, well it's sure an attractive body, rope the marks in. And a nice body symphony to go with it, rhythmic heart beats, contented stomach rumbles. To be bodies: recordings and pictures of hideous, aged, diseased bodies farting, pissing, shitting, groaning, dying. To do everything: a man in a filthy apartment surrounded by unpaid bills, unanswered letters, jumps up and starts washing dishes and writing letters. To do nothing: he slumps in a chair, jumps up, slumps in chair, jumps up. Finally, slumps in a chair, drooling in idiot helplessness, while he looks at the disorder piled around him. The reactive mind commands can also be used to advantage with illness tapes. While projecting past cold sore on to the subject's face, and playing back to him a past illness tape, you can say: to be me, to be you, to stay here, to stay there, to be a body, to be bodies, to stay in, to stay out, to stay present, to stay absent. To what extent are these reactive mind phrases when scrambled effective in causing disagreeable symptoms in control volunteer subjects? As to Mr. Hubbard's claims for the reactive mind, only research can give us the answers.

The RM then is an artifact designed to limit and stultify on a mass scale. In order to have this effect it must be widely implanted. This can readily be done with modern electronic equipment and the techniques described in this treatise. The RM consists of commands which seem harmless and in fact unavoidable ... To be a body ... but which can have the most horrific consequences.

Here are some sample RM screen effects ...

As the theater darkens a bright light appears on the left side of the screen. The screen lights up

To be nobody ... On screen shadow of ladder and soldier incinerated by the Hiroshima blast

To be everybody ... Street crowds, riots, panics

To be me ... A beautiful girl and a handsome young man point to selves

To be you ... They point to audience ...

Hideous hags and old men, lepers, drooling idiots point to themselves and to the audience as they intone ...

To be me

To be you

Command no. 5 ... To be myself

Command no. 6 ... To be others

On screen a narcotics officer is addressing an audience of school boys. Spread out on a table in front of him are syringes, kief pipes, samples of heroin, hashiesh, LSD.

Officer: 'Five trips on a drug can be a pleasant and exciting experience ...'

On screen young trippers ... 'I'm really myself for the first time'

ETC happy trips ... To be myself ... no. 5 ...

Officer: 'THE SIXTH WILL PROBABLY BLOW YOUR HEAD OFF'

Shot shows a man blowing his head off with a shotgun in his mouth ...

Officer: 'Like a 15-year-old boy I knew until recently, you

could well end up dying in your own spew ... To be others
no.6 ...

To be an animal ... A lone Wolf Scout ...

To be animals: He joins other wolf scouts playing,
laughing, shouting

To be an animal ... Bestial and ugly human behavior ...
brawls, disgusting eating and sex scenes

To be animals ... Cows, sheep and pigs driven to the
slaughter house

To be a body

To be bodies

A beautiful body ... a copulating couple ... Cut back and
forth and run on seven-second loop for several minutes ...
scramble at different speeds ... Audience must be made to
realize that to be a body is to be bodies ... A body exists to be
other bodies

To be a body ... Death scenes and recordings ... a scramble
of last words

To be bodies ... Vista of cemeteries ...

To do it now ... Couple embracing hotter and hotter

To do it now ... A condemned cell ... Condemned man is
same actor as lover ... He is led away by the guards screaming
and struggling. Cut back and forth between sex scene and
man led to execution. Couple in sex scene have orgasm as the
condemned man is hanged, electrocuted, gassed, garrotted,
shot in the head with a pistol

To do it later ... The couple pull away ... One wants to go
out and eat and go to a show or something ... They put on
their hats ...

To do it later ... Warden arrives at condemned cell to tell
the prisoner he has a stay of execution

To do it now ... Grim faces in the Pentagon. Strategic is on
its way ... Well THIS IS IT ... This sequence cut in with sex
scenes and a condemned man led to execution, culminates in
execution, orgasm, nuclear explosion ... The condemned lover
is a horribly burned survivor

To do it later ... 1920 walk out sequence to 'The Sunny Side
of the Street' ... A disappointed general turns from the phone

to say the President has opened top level hot wire talks with Russia and China ... Condemned man gets another stay of execution

To be an animal ... One lemming busily eating lichen ...

To be animals ... Hordes of lemmings swarming all over each other in mounting hysteria ... A pile of drowned lemmings in front of somebody's nice little cottage on a Finnish lake where he is methodically going through sex positions with his girl friend. They wake up in a stink of dead lemmings

To be an animal ... Little boy put on pot

To be animals ... The helpless shitting infant is eaten alive by rats

To stay put ... a man has just been hanged. The doctor steps forward with a stethoscope

To stay down ... Body is carried out with the rope around neck ... naked corpse on the autopsy table ... corpse buried in quicklime

To stay up ... Erect phallus

To stay down ... White man burns off a Negro's genitals with blow torch ... Theater darkens into the blow torch on left side of the screen

To stay present

To stay absent

To stay present ... A boy masturbates in front of sex pictures ... Cut to face of white man who is burning off black genitals with blow torch

To stay absent ... Sex phantasies of the boy ... The black slumps dead with genitals burned off and intestines popping out

To stay present ... Boy watches strip tease, intent, fascinated ... A man stands on trap about to be hanged

To stay present ... Sex phantasies of the boy 'I pronounce this man dead'

To stay present ... Boy whistles at girl in street ... A man's body twists in the electric chair, his leg hairs crackling with blue fire

To stay absent ... Boy sees himself in bed with girl ... Man slumps dead in chair smoke curling from under the hood saliva dripping from his mouth ... ,

The Theater lights up. In the sky a plane over Hiroshima ... Little Boy slides out

To stay present ... The plane, the pilot, the American flag ...

To stay absent ... Theater darkens into atomic blast on screen.

Here we see ordinary men and women going about their ordinary everyday jobs and diversions ... subways, streets, buses, trains, airports, stations, waiting rooms, homes, flats, restaurants, offices, factories ... working, eating, playing, defecating, making love

A chorus of voices cuts in RM phrases

To stay up

To stay down

Elevators, airports, stairs, ladders

To stay in

To stay out

Street signs, door signs, people at heads of lines admitted to restaurants and theaters

To be myself

To be others

Customs agents check passports, man identifies himself at bank to cash check

To stay present

To stay absent

People watching films, reading, looking at TV ...

A composite of this sound and image track is now run on seven second loop without change for several minutes.

Now cut in the horror pictures

To stay up

To stay down

Elevators, airports, stairs, ladders, hangings, castrations

To stay in

To stay out

Door signs, operation scenes ... doctor tosses bloody tonsils, adenoids, appendix into receptacle

To stay present
To stay absent
People watching film ... ether mask, ether vertigo ...
triangles, spheres, rectangles, pyramids, prisms, coils go away
and come in in regular sequence ... a coil coming in, two coils
coming in, three coils coming in ... a coil going away, two coils
going away, four going away

A coil straight ahead going away, two coils on the left and
right going away, three coils left right and center going away,
four coils right left center and behind going away

A coil coming, two coils coming in, three coils coming in,
four coils coming in ... spirals of light ... round and round
faster faster, baby eaten by rats, hangings, electrocutions,
castrations ...

The RM can be cut in with the most ordinary scenes
covering the planet in a smog of fear ...

The RM is a built-in electronic police force armed with
hideous threats. You don't want to be a cute little wolf cub?
All right, cattle to the slaughter house meat on a hook.

Here is a nostalgic reconstruction of the old-fashioned Mayan methods. The wrong kind of workers with wrong thoughts are tortured to death in rooms under the pyramid ... A young worker has been given a powerful hallucinogen and sexual stimulant ... Naked he is strapped down and skinned alive ... The dark Gods of pain are surfacing from the immemorial filth of time ... The Ouab Bird stands there, screams, watching through his wild blue eyes. Others are crabs from the waist up clicking their claws in ecstasy, they dance around and mimic the flayed man. The scribes are busy with sketches ... Now he is strapped into a segmented copper centipede and placed gently on a bed of hot coals ... Soon the priests will dig the soft meat from the shell with their golden claws ... Here is another youth staked out on an ant hill honey smeared on his eyes and genitals ... Others with heavy weights on their backs are slowly dragged through wooden troughs in which shards of obsidian have been driven ... So the priests are the masters of pain and fear and death ... To do right ... To obey the priests ... To do wrong? The priests' very presence and a few banal words ...

The priests postulated and set up an hermetic universe of which they were the axiomatic controllers. In so doing they became Gods who controlled the known universe of the workers. They became Fear and Pain, Death and Time. By making opposition seemingly impossible they failed to make any provision for opposition. There is evidence that this control system broke down in some areas before the arrival of the White God. Stellae have been found defaced and overturned, mute evidence of a worker's revolution. How did this happen? The history of revolutionary movements shows that they are usually led by defectors from the ruling class. The Spanish rule in South America was overthrown by Spanish revolutionaries. The French were driven out of Algeria by Algerians educated in France. Perhaps one of the priest-gods defected and organized a worker's revolution ...

The priest-gods in the temple. They move very slowly, faces ravaged with age and disease. Parasitic worms infest their dead fibrous flesh. They are making calculations from the sacred books.

'400,000,000 years ago on this day a grievous thing happened ...'

Limestone skulls rain in through the porticos. The Young Maize God leads the workers as they storm the temple and drag the priests out. They build a huge brush fire, throw the priests in and then throw the sacred books in after them. Time buckles and bends. The old Gods, surfacing from the immemorial depths of time, burst in the sky ... Mr. Hart stands there looking at the broken stelae ... 'How did this happen?'

His control system must be absolute and worldwide. Because such a control system is even more vulnerable to attack from without than revolt from within ... Here is Bishop Landa burning the sacred books. To give you an idea as to what is happening, imagine our civilization invaded by louts from outer space ...

'Get some bulldozers in here. Clear out all this crap ...' The formulae of all the natural sciences, books, paintings, the lot, swept into a vast pile and burned. And that's it. No one ever heard of it ...

Three codices survived the vandalism of Bishop Landa and these are burned around the edges. No way to know if we have here the sonnets of Shakespeare, the Mona Lisa or the remnants of a Sears Roebuck catalogue after the old out-house burned down in a brush fire. A whole civilization went up in smoke ...

When the Spaniards arrived, they found the Mayan aristocrats lolling in hammocks. Well, time to show them what is what. Five captured workers, bound and stripped, are castrated on a tree stump, the bleeding, sobbing, screaming bodies thrown into a pile ...

'And now get this through your gook nuts. We want to see a pile of gold that big and we want to see it pronto. The White God has spoken.'

Consider now the human voice as a weapon. To what extent can the unaided human voice duplicate effects that can be done with a tape recorder? Learning to speak with the mouth shut, thus displacing your speech, is fairly easy. You can also learn to speak backwards, which is fairly difficult. I have seen people who can repeat what you are saying after you and finish at the same time. This is a most disconcerting trick, particularly when practiced on a mass scale at a political rally. Is it possible to actually scramble speech? A far-reaching biologic weapon can be forged from a new language. In fact such a language already exists. It exists as Chinese, a total language closer to the multi-level structure of experience, with a script derived from hieroglyphs, more closely related to the objects and areas described. The equanimity of the Chinese is undoubtedly derived from their language being structured for greater sanity. I notice the Chinese, wherever they are, retain the written and spoken language, while other immigrant peoples will lose their language in two generations. The aim of this project is to build a language in which certain falsifications inherent in all existing Western languages will be made incapable of formulation. The following falsifications to be deleted from the proposed language:

The IS of Identity. You are an animal. You are a body. Now whatever you may be you are not an 'animal', you are not a 'body', because these are verbal labels. The IS of identity always carries the implication of that and nothing else, and it also carries the assignment of permanent condition. To stay that way. All naming calling presupposes the IS of identity.

This concept is unnecessary in a hieroglyphic language like ancient Egyptian and in fact frequently omitted. No need to say the sun IS in the sky, sun in sky suffices. The verb *to be* can easily be omitted from any language and the followers of Count Korzybski have done this, eliminating the verb *to be* in English. However, it is difficult to tidy up the English language by arbitrary exclusion of concepts which remain in force so long as the unchanged language is spoken.

The definite article THE. THE contains the implication of one and only: THE God, THE universe, THE way, THE right, THE wrong. If there is another, then THAT universe, THAT way is no longer THE universe, THE way. The definite article THE will be deleted and the indefinite article A will take its place.

The whole concept of EITHER/OR. Right or wrong, physical or mental, true or false, the whole concept of OR will be deleted from the language and replaced by juxtaposition, by *and*. This is done to some extent in any pictorial language where the two concepts stand literally side by side. These falsifications inherent in English and other Western alphabetical languages give the reactive mind commands their overwhelming force in the languages. Consider the IS of identity. When I say to be me, to be you, to be myself, to be others – whatever I may be called upon to be or say that I am – I am not the verbal label 'myself'. I cannot be and am not the verbal label 'myself'. The word BE in English contains, as a virus contains, its precoded message of damage, the categorical imperative of permanent condition. To be a body, to be nothing else, to stay a body. To be an animal, to be nothing else, to stay an animal. If you see the relation of the I to the body, as the relation of a pilot to his ship, you see the full crippling force of the reactive mind command to be a body. Telling the pilot to be the plane, then who will pilot the plane?

The IS of identity, assigning a rigid and permanent status, was greatly reinforced by the customs and passport control that came in after World War I. Whatever you may be, you are not the verbal labels in your passport any more than you are the word 'self'. So you must be prepared to prove at all times that you are what you are not. Much of the force of the reactive mind also depends on the falsification inherent in the categorical definite article THE. THE now, THE past, THE time, THE space, THE energy, THE matter, THE universe. Definite article THE contains the implication of no other. THE universe locks you in THE, and denies the possibility of any other. If other universes are possible, then the universe is no longer THE it becomes A. The definite article THE in the proposed language is deleted and replaced by A. Many of the RM commands are in point of fact contradictory commands and a contradictory command gains its force from the Aristotelian concept of either/or. To do everything, to do nothing, to have everything, to have nothing, to do it all, to do not any, to stay up, to stay down, to stay in, to stay out, to stay present, to stay absent. These are in point of fact either/or propositions. To do nothing *or* everything, to have it all *or* not any, to stay present *or* to stay absent. Either/or is more difficult to formulate in a written language where both alternatives are pictorially represented and can be deleted entirely from the spoken language. The whole reactive mind can be in fact reduced to three little words – to be 'THE'. That is to be what you are not, verbal formulations.

I have frequently spoken of word and image as viruses or as acting as viruses, and this is not an allegorical comparison. It will be seen that the falsifications in syllabic Western languages are in point of fact actual virus mechanisms. The IS of identity is in point of fact the virus mechanism. If we can infer purpose from behavior, then the purpose of a virus is TO SURVIVE. To survive at any expense to the host invaded. To be an animal, to be a body. To be an animal body that the virus can invade. To be animals, to be bodies. To be more animal bodies so that the virus can move from one body to another. To stay present as an animal body, to stay absent as antibody or resistance to the body invasion.

The categorical THE is also a virus mechanism, locking you in THE virus universe. EITHER/OR is another virus formula. It is always you OR the virus. EITHER/OR. This is in point of fact the conflict formula which is seen to be an archetypical virus mechanism. The proposed language will delete these virus mechanisms and make them impossible of formulation in the language. The language will be a tonal language like Chinese, it will also have a hieroglyphic script as pictorial as possible without being too cumbersome or difficult to write. This language will give one the option of silence. When not talking, the user of this language can take in the silent images of the written, pictorial and symbol languages.

I have described here a number of weapons and tactics in the war game. Weapons that change consciousness could call the war game in question. All games are hostile. Basically there is only one game and that game is war. It's the old army game from here to eternity. Mr. Hubbard says that Scientology is a game where everybody wins. There are no games where everybody wins. That's what games are all about, winning and losing ... The Versailles Treaty ... Hitler dances the Occupation Jig ... War criminals hang at Nuremberg ... It is a rule of this game that there can be no final victory since this would mean the end of the war game. Yet every player must believe in final victory and strive for it with all his power. Faced by the nightmare of final defeat he has no alternative. So all existing technologies with escalating efficiency produce more and more total weapons until we have the atom bomb which could end the game by destroying all players. Now mock up a miracle. The so stupid players decide to save the game. They sit down around a big table and draw up a plan for the immediate deactivation and eventual destruction of all atomic weapons. Why stop there? Conventional bombs are unnecessarily destructive if nobody else has them hein? Let's turn the war clock back to 1917:

> Keep the home fires burning
> Though the hearts are yearning
> There's a long, long trail awinding ...
> Back to the American Civil War ...

'He has loosed the fatal lightning of his terrible swift sword.' His fatal lightning didn't cost as much in those days. Save a lot on the defense budget this way on back to flintlocks, matchlocks, swords, armor, lances, bows and arrows, spears, stone axes and clubs. Why stop there? Why not grow teeth and claws, poison fangs, stingers, spines, quills, beaks and suckers and stink glands and fight it out in the muck hein?

That is what this revolution is about. End of game. New games? There are no new games from here to eternity. END OF THE WAR GAME.